BOOK ONE

A NOVEL BY

A. LAWRENCE

For Cindy,
who encouraged me from the beginning.

Contents

Chapter 1: Ghost Town

Shay tried to quietly bounce her heel against the pavement. If she was too loud Max would have to start all over and they would be absolutely insufferable about it.

"The Johnson House." Max used their serious camera work voice. "A regular house, on a regular street, but something dark lurks behind the windows."

Something dark was definitely behind the blinds, shut tight against the outside world. Shay was pretty confident it had more to do with the electricity being off than anything remotely paranormal.

"Tonight, I've been asked to investigate what could have terrified a mild-mannered suburban family so badly that they moved several hundred miles away without warning. Welcome…to Ghost Town."

Shay waited a beat so Max could edit her out. "Boooo. I still object to that name."

"That's fine, it's my show." Max held out a hand to her and she accepted, letting them haul her to her feet. Even standing Max was a good head taller than her, but most people were. "Well, you ready to go in?"

"I guess," she said. "You really think this place is haunted?"

"Maybe." Max squinted up at it.

"Are you going to cry like you did in that barn?" Shay asked with a slight grin.

Their glare was colder than the late October air. "That owl came for my face, Shay. It wasn't funny."

"Oh, it was pretty funny," Shay said. She nudged Max lightly with her elbow when they continued to sulk. "Hey, if you had been in actual danger, I would have punched that owl myself. With my bare fists. To defend your honor and your perfect face. Now c'mon, let's go explore a haunted house."

She supposed if any house on the block was haunted, it had to be the one they were standing in front of. It was dark blue, or at least it had been. The paint was worn and weathered. Rust stains blossomed down from the gutter. The lawn was coated with dead leaves. The trees up and down the street were still clinging to their fall splendor, but in front of the Johnson House they were bare, branches forming a lattice of clawed, bony hands reaching for a dull, overcast sky. A "For Sale" sign was sunk deeply next to the sidewalk.

It wasn't the rust stains on the siding or the lawn that made the house foreboding. Some other quality was making her feel cold.

Maybe it was just the wind rushing down the street, clattering leaves across the sidewalk. She shivered, huddling deeper into her hoodie. The for-sale sign creaked. A smiling woman had been plastered on it, but water stains had marred her smile and her eyes had been scratched into starbursts of white.

"Okay, gonna record again." Max held up their phone and went back to their video voice, which was only a little more sinister than their normal voice. At least, that was what Shay thought they were going for. They just sounded vaguely British to her. "It's been two years since the Johnsons picked up and moved out in a single night. No one knows why. The house has stood empty ever since, but sometimes a strange glow can be seen behind the blinds. Teen vandals? Or is it something more sinister? No one has ever investigated, but we have been given the green light to go in this evening and see if we can find out what terror has gripped the house."

Shay laughed the moment it was safe to. "Something more sinister than teen vandals? Have you met any?"

"I've met you," Max said.

Shay gasped, pretending to be scandalized. "That is so rude. You know I have never vandalized anything."

"Just my life, then," they sighed.

"Shut up, you love me."

"Unfortunately for me," Max said. They pulled a key out of their hoodie pocket. "Quiet, I want to get us walking up to the house."

"If you insist."

Their shoes crunched on the driveway, the cement pitted and cracked. Max turned the camera to her and she gave them a cheesy smile and a thumbs up that had them grinning.

The Great Ghost Debate had started in middle school. Max was a believer. Shay wasn't, and didn't particularly care, but Max got so riled up about it that she pretended she did.

It had mattered more to them than she realized. At some point, while she was away for college, Max had taken to filming videos of dubious quality with their phone. They were even starting to gain a decent amount of followers. She'd opted to tag along when she moved back, mostly to keep Max from scaring themself into cardiac arrest over a weird shadow in a corner.

And it was more entertaining than just sitting around at home, hoping someone would like her resume enough to call her back.

Max opened the screen door. The hinges screeched out a protest. They had to get their hip in the way to keep it propped open. They unlocked the wooden door behind it and stepped back, looking at her.

She stared at them. "What?"

"After you." Max made a sweeping gesture inside.

"Oh, you suck," Shay said.

"You shouldn't have brought up the owl."

She huffed at them. "If something jumps on my face, I swear I will never, ever forgive you."

"Gonna take my chances." Max grinned at her.

"I guess we wouldn't want more owls trying to steal your face," Shay conceded, shouldering past them a little more roughly than necessary.

The door was heavy, and she had to shove at it with her shoulder. It must have warped in the frame. The musty smell of a room that had been shut too long rolled out onto the porch.

It took her eyes a moment to adjust to the dimness. She toggled the light switch next to the door, but nothing happened.

"You really think that would work?" Max asked.

"I absolutely did," Shay said. "I was going to ruin your whole show by paying the electric bill for two years on a house I've never heard of. Guess my plan is ruined."

"Ha."

The entryway led to a set of stairs, the kitchen farther on and the living room immediately to her left. It was just an empty square of painted walls and carpet. Muddy footprints formed paths between indents still left over from where furniture must have sat.

She walked into the kitchen. The cabinets and island in the center were just shapes in the gloom before she pulled out her phone to use as a flashlight. The room filled with cold light, the shadows substantial enough to cut. A few cabinets had been left hanging open, one door hanging by a single hinge.

The only things on the island were a few extremely dead houseplants in ugly flowerpots and an equally dead beetle, its legs curled up tightly

"Aw sleep well, sweet prince."

"What was that?" Max asked.

"Nothing!" she called back, realizing she couldn't possibly explain. She checked the open cupboards, but there was only more dust inside.

There was something about empty houses that left Shay feeling off. It wasn't a ghost thing: she'd been in plenty of supposedly haunted places and had never experienced anything paranormal. The idea of someone living somewhere, then leaving behind an empty shell of their life, felt like tripping on nothing. It had been that way when her parents sold her childhood home and they'd stood in front of it for the last time after a flurry of cleaning, trying to find whatever had washed up in the corners. Or when they'd moved from the apartment before that, with its sad brown carpet and empty white walls, though she barely remembered it.

A sadness, nostalgia, and something else she couldn't ever describe. Something that washed over her even when she left the bare walls of the dorm room that she had never really thought of as home.

Kitchens were the worst. They were the center of life, the heart of a home, where meals were cooked and families gathered.

Without that, a house felt gutted and dead.

Maybe it was that feeling that made so many people think that empty places were haunted.

"What do you see?" Max's voice broke through her thoughts. "Did you get eaten by owls?"

"The owls want to carry me off and make me their queen, actually. No luck so far. This place is great! We can move in right away. Even comes with its own dead plants, and a bug," Shay said. "The bug is dead, too. Just in case that was a concern."

"Not really." Max finally joined her in the kitchen. "Here, save your phone battery."

They handed her a thin, metal flashlight. She clicked it on and swept the beam over the cupboards, throwing them into much higher clarity than her phone had managed. "Oh, this is new. I can't tell if we're moving forward or backwards. This feels so fresh and exciting and yet so retro."

"I just didn't want my phone to die again." Max sounded a little put out and she knew she'd laid it on too thick. "Besides, if anything is retro, it's your phone."

She patted their shoulder and let the comment about her ancient phone slide. "Thanks. This was really nice of you to get."

"I know," Max said. "I'll have my secretary send you the bill."

"Ooh, he's going to be so disappointed when I send in that IOU," Shay teased back. Falling into the familiar territory of joking with Max eased some of the tension in her shoulders. It didn't do anything for the headache starting to pound behind one eye.

"Didn't know my imaginary secretary was a man."

"It's equality."

"Ugh, do you feel that?" Max shuddered and stepped a little closer to her.

"Kinda chilly, yeah, but the heat hasn't been on for a while," Shay said. Cold air pressed around her. The house must have had poor insulation. She wasn't too surprised given the state of the outside.

"The air feels heavy," Max said.

Shay nodded, that one she agreed with. "Sure, kind of stale. Anyway, I'm going to check for random wildlife, you can do your EVP or whatever you need to."

"Yeah, good idea," Max agreed.

She left them to ask the empty kitchen questions like: "Is there someone here with us? Do you have unfinished business? Are you aware, sir, that you are, in fact, a ghost?" and continued her solo tour of the house. All she found was dust and a large spider in the downstairs bathroom. She shut the door behind her just in case. The sun was setting outside, the house growing darker. She finished with the first floor and sat down on the staircase, waiting for Max to be done. A cold draft wafted its way from above. She made a note that it was time to wear a real coat to investigations.

Max was nearing the end of their script when she heard the footsteps.

They were loud and heavy, like a large, angry man was pacing down the hall. A shiver that had nothing to do with the temperature worked its way up her spine. She stood up and took a step back towards the door, eyeing the top of the stairs. It was lost to gloom. She tried her flashlight, but it didn't catch anything. If anyone was upstairs, they stayed hidden.

"Did you hear that?" Max came out of the kitchen to stand next to her.

"I thought we were the first to investigate?" Shay looked up at them.

"We are, I don't know what that was." Max's voice switched back to their official one. "We just heard the sound of footsteps coming from upstairs, even though the house is locked and we're supposed to be the only ones here. Could this be the house settling? Or could it be what drove the family out of their home? We're going upstairs to investigate now."

"We are?" Shay asked.

"I am," Max amended.

"And if that was a person?" She didn't like how it had sounded. If she had been squatting in a house and two ghost hunters came in, she wouldn't have gone stomping down the hallway.

Unease was not mixing well with the pain that was getting worse. The sooner they finished their investigation, the sooner she could lie down in a dark room with a compress over her eyes.

"On second thought, let's just come back later," Max said. "You're getting a headache."

She knew they were just concerned. She'd been getting headaches off and on for months, of course they had every right to be worried. She should just be happy that they noticed.

She just wanted things to be normal. "I'm fine. I'm great, actually. Feeling awesome. We're going to go upstairs and I'm going to hit some guy with my flashlight. Or it was just the house settling."

"Shay—"

"I'm going!"

She walked up the stairs before they could argue. Her fingers hurt from gripping the flashlight. Each step felt colder than the last. There was a door at the top of the stairs, white and nondescript. She swung the light, the shadows on either side lurching and jumping. Her heart was beating in her ears.

A soft scrape, to the left.

She darted the beam towards it, but she couldn't see anything beyond the edge of the wall.

"Okay, I've moved on from kind of worried to actually freaked out," Max admitted in a quiet, small voice. They were only two steps behind her. She hadn't even heard them moving. Maybe they'd had the right idea, thinking they should come back later. "We should go."

"No, we're investigators, so we investigate," Shay said, even though she wanted nothing more than to turn and run down the stairs herself. She really wished she'd taken the baseball bat her brother had offered. She'd stupidly said it wouldn't work on ghosts.

Maybe she could throw her ancient phone at whoever it was and run.

She reached the top of the stairs and shrieked.

Chapter 2: The Mirror

"What is it?" Max charged up the stairs after her. They could be very brave when it mattered.

Or didn't matter, in this case. "Sorry! Sorry. There's a mirror and for a second I thought it was a person… and it was, but it was just me. Whoo! That was way too exciting."

"Oh." Max looked at the mirror and gave her a sly grin. "And you made fun of the owl thing."

"We heard possible footsteps. I thought it was a person, just standing there, staring in the dark." Shay put a hand to her chest. "Oh man, my heart is still going crazy. Is this how you feel, like, all the time?"

"Maybe." Max shrugged. "Are you okay?"

"Wow. I am so sorry, this sucks, but it's kind of like a punch to the chest," Shay said. The rush of fear and adrenaline had left her feeling giddy. "No wonder you believe in this stuff. It's like crack."

"That's not-"

"Ghost crack." Shay gave them finger guns.

Max sighed. "Look, I'm really glad you're okay and not being attacked by ghosts or random strangers. And that no one is up here."

"I guess not," she conceded, though she could have sworn she heard something. It must have been the house settling. Or Max was finally getting to her.

"I'll have to check the audio later."

"You mean you'll have to reflect on it."

She couldn't really see their face with how dark it was, but she could nearly feel their eyes rolling. "Sure. I'll have to do that."

The hallway was lined with closed doors. Max turned their phone to the door right at the top of the stairs. "It looks like no one is up here, so what were the mysterious footsteps we just heard? It sounded like a large person, but neither of us heard a door close, so it's likely all of the rooms are empty. We're going to open the first door. Shay, do you want to do the honors?"

"Will do," Shay said. That must have been the theme of the episode, Max making her do everything first. The owl must have scared them more than she thought. Or it was revenge for laughing until she cried over the entire incident.

It was a coat closet.

The floor was littered with white plastic hangers. A few of them still hung from the beam, like someone had grabbed an armful of coats and left whatever they couldn't easily carry behind. A snowboarding glove lay on the ground like a dead spider.

Shay giggled. "We're really setting the bar in here."

"Are you done?" Max gave her a few more seconds to cackle about it.

"I'm just getting the hang of it." Shay grinned at them. They didn't bother replying. "Do you think I'm coating it on? I would glove to have your opinion."

"Well, my opinion is now that you're done being a jerk-" they paused while she snickered. "Great. Good. Anyway, look. The closet still has stuff in it. That's weird. You have to admit that's weird."

"Yeah, now you're basketing the right questions." Shay shone her light on a basket on the second shelf.

"Oh my god. That's it. I'm leaving you here."

"Okay, fine, I'm shutting the door on this conversation." She closed the closet door. Max turned towards the stairs and she grabbed their hood before they could leave her. "No! I'm done! For real this time. Next door?"

"Next door." Max nodded. "But now you have to open all of them."

"If I get killed by a guy stealing pipes out of the walls, I'm going to make ghosts real. So I can haunt you."

The second room was another bathroom. Her flashlight glinted off of the mirror, throwing their reflections into silhouettes. The shadows slid across the walls and for a moment Shay thought she saw the shape of a person, but Max didn't say anything.

Decorative towels hung over the toilet. The bathmat was askew on the floor and the shower curtain half open. There was even soap next to the sink, covered in a thick layer of gray dust.

"Need to wash your hands?"

"After being in here? Desperately," Max said.

The other rooms were bedrooms, each one with an unmade bed, open dresser drawers hurriedly dumped out and left hanging open. Clothes, books, and all manner of personal items were left strewn across the floor, frozen in a moment of complete disarray.

"Okay, so, yeah, this is weird," Shay admitted. It felt like someone had put a cold hand to the back of her neck. "Like actually spooky. You get the creepy award for this one."

"So glad I was recording that," Max said.

"Shut up, it's just really weird." Shay shoved her hands into the pockets of her hoodie. "And it's cold. And I keep thinking I see something out of the corner of my eye."

Max perked up. "Really?"

"Yeah, just shadows, though," she said. "Probably our shadows. Still not my favorite."

"It is actually a lot colder up here," Max admitted. "Lemme switch over to EMF readings…"

"Someday, I'm going to get you real ghost hunting equipment," Shay told them.

"An EMF detector is like sixty bucks online."

"Someday I'm going to get you a gift card to put towards real ghost hunting equipment."

"That's what I thought," Max said. "But I am glad you think ghost hunting equipment is real."

"Real as in 'not messing with your phone'." Shay closed the last door. Clothes had hemorrhaged out of the closet and the bed sheets were still halfway on the mattress. The skin between her shoulder blades prickled uncomfortably.

"No super high readings on the EMF." Max ignored her. "I'm going to go ahead and put away the EMF reader, since I have no idea what could still have batteries and mess with my readings. The sun did set so a temperature drop is expected, but it is getting really cold in here. Forty-seven degrees and dropping."

"Crappy insulation," Shay said, because she felt like she had to.

"Maybe." Max didn't look convinced and she really couldn't blame them. "Let's turn off the lights for a moment."

"Are you serious?" Shay had to make sure, but Max was already clicking off their light. "Max. No. This is a terrible idea."

"But ghosts aren't real, Shay, we'll be fine."

"Max, please don't use my words against me, it makes me feel bad." Shay turned off her flashlight, too. They stood in the doorway to the master bedroom. Orange light seeped through gaps in the blinds from the lamp outside. It flickered a few times. A car passed by on the street, the hiss of its tires like whispering.

"Is there anyone here with us?" Max asked, voice quiet.

A creak answered them. They both looked towards the source at the end of the hall, but the door at the end was closed.

"Is there something you want to say? I'm listening," Max said.

Another creak from the end of the hallway. Shay shifted a little closer to Max. They weren't the bravest, but their presence was comforting, anyway.

"Well." Max squared their shoulders. "I guess that means it's time to check out the attic. Anything could happen, so stay tuned."

"It is pretty dark, and if it's as tidy as these rooms we could trip," Shay said. "So, I'll give you that."

"Oh, let's just go." Max grabbed her wrist and pulled her down the hall. They stopped and she nearly ran into them. "That door was closed, wasn't it?"

She looked around them. The door was open a few inches. Beyond it was a set of stairs that turned and disappeared beyond the door jamb.

"It must have been, I saw the mirror," she said.

"Bad latch?" Max suggested.

Sometimes Shay was scared during an investigation, not that she told Max. They were usually in dark places where anything could happen, and she was only human.

Something about this place made her want to believe in ghosts. It felt less scary than someone breaking and entering or a gas leak. A gas leak could be responsible for her head feeling like it might burst, but she didn't think it could explain away the footsteps.

Instead of saying any of that, she shrugged. "Or… someone is here with us. And I don't mean a ghost, I mean a living breathing type of person. If someone is up here with us…I'm not about that, Max. Haunted houses? Whatever. Occupied houses? Absolutely not."

"There shouldn't be anyone else here," Max said. "The door was locked, remember?"

"The front door, sure," Shay said. "But there were a bunch of windows at ground level, anyone could have slipped through one. And we heard someone walking around. I think they're up there."

As if to prove her point there was a single, heavy footstep.

"We should go," Shay said.

"I don't think that's a person." Max had gone as pale as their dark complexion allowed. "I dunno. I'm scared, too. If you don't want to go up there that's fine, we can go. It's okay."

She knew they weren't trying to insinuate she was too scared to go up. If she said she wanted to go, she knew that they wouldn't say anything. They would just go.

Her pride would take a beating.

It was just one small set of stairs, and they could always run for the front door.

"No, you're right, it's probably just raccoons or something." She nodded. "Really fat raccoons. Okay. Let's go up there, and if it's not local wildlife we run. Plan?"

"And if it's a ghost?" Max asked.

"Then you have proof, either way we're not dead?" Shay walked past them, trying to ignore the fear crawling up her throat. "And if it's a murderer-"

"I'll make sure to get murdered, too, so we can be ghost buds," Max said.

"You'd better." She reached the door and pushed it the rest of the way open. There was a thin layer of mist on the steps, pouring down them like the world's slowest waterfall. It was almost green in the beam of her flashlight. The temperature plummeted. Someone must have left a window open.

That, or Max's friends were upstairs with a bucket of dry ice, waiting to have a good laugh at her. Which was probably fair, but she was already prepared to be very upset with them.

"I don't like this." Max grabbed her hood.

She stepped down on the first stair and her flashlight went out.

"Oh, c'mon." She banged it against her thigh, but probably just gave herself bruises for her troubles. Max's flashlight cut out a second later, leaving them both standing in the dark.

"My phone!" They let go of her hood, stabbing the button frantically. "Seriously? I had tons of battery left!"

"I'll record for you." She pulled out her phone. The blank screen didn't respond to her touch. "Well, that's less weird than yours, but-"

Blue light flooded the space above them, shining through the railing. Bars of light and shadow stretched up against the wall.

Shay felt like she was in a dream, walking up the last few steps. The mist was cold enough she could have been wading through icy water.

The attic was a single, long room, stretching the length of the house. The ceiling sloped with the roof. Boxes and old furniture softened the edges, but the center was clear, leading to a mirror propped up against the window at the far end.

It had a heavily curled frame, like the ones she saw in the windows of antique stores that Max wouldn't go into. The way it was angled, it should have been reflecting the ceiling.

The surface was glowing.

"Another mirror?" Max stepped a little closer to her. She hadn't even realized they'd followed her up the stairs.

"I mean, kind of. Trick of the light, maybe?" Shay said. She looked behind them to see if there was a light for the mirror to catch. There was no window above the stairs. "No one's here."

"I don't think so?" Max's voice had gone squeaky with fear. She couldn't blame them, she was shaking and she knew it wasn't entirely from the cold. Her head hurt so badly she squeezed one eye closed to alleviate the pressure. It didn't help.

The mirror went black with such suddenness that Max screamed, nearly pulling them both down the stairs when they backed up.

The attic door slammed shut.

"Time to go!" Max ran down the stairs, nearly tripping. They grabbed the doorknob and yelped. "It's freezing!"

Shay reached past them, yanking her sleeve over her hand. The doorknob was a lump of ice under her hand, the cold burning through her sleeve. It wouldn't even rattle. "It's stuck!"

"Turn it!" Max yelled, like it would help.

"I told you, it's stuck, I can't!"

Wind howled through the room. Max and Shay locked eyes for a second. She stepped back and they hit the door with their shoulder. The howl grew louder and higher, turning into a scream. Shay's hair whipped around her face. Fog cascaded through the railing. She pressed her hands to her ears but it did nothing to block out the sound piercing through her brain.

Max stepped back and the wind stopped. The silence was thick and suffocating in its absence.

"Shay?" Max's voice was practically inaudible.

The fog was nearly to her waist. She was so cold her teeth were chattering. Max grabbed her hand and hauled her up a few steps to get her out of it. Her feet were numb and she stumbled on the stairs.

The mirror was still black, the edges glowing a dull, greenish blue. The room was blurry and distorted, as if she was looking at it through a funhouse mirror. Every few seconds her headache seemed to make the distortion worse. She rubbed her eyes under her glasses like it would help.

Everything snapped back into focus.

Her headache, which felt like it was about to split her skull, died down to a dull pressure behind her eyes.

Whispering filled the space around them. Or maybe the sound of static.

"What's happening?" Max squeezed her hand, a little too tightly. She did the same back.

She couldn't answer them. She felt strange, like a rubber band that had been stretched too far and snapped back. Her throat hurt like she had been screaming, but her headache was clearing.

A skeletal hand reached from inside the mirror and grabbed the frame.

Chapter 3: Skeleton

The whispering rose in volume, so loud she wanted to cover her ears. She was so frozen the simple motion felt impossible.

Her brain was still screeching about impossibilities of special effects when a man pulled himself through the mirror's surface.

He stood in front of the still dark mirror, all in shades of blue. With a shock she realized she could see it through him, like looking through a sheet of old, wavy glass. His head was bowed, his features masked by the wide brim of a top hat. He was tall and gaunt, in a tailored pinstripe suit and tails, fading to nothing closer to the floor.

He straightened.

The room went silent.

Under the brim of the hat was a skull. One hollow socket was covered by a monocle.

Shay was too afraid to scream.

He turned to the side, as if listening for something. She could see the barest hint of a spectral face floating in front of the skull – a nose, the curve of a cheek, the barest glint of an eye.

When he looked at her again the face was gone. The rictus grin was trained in her direction.

Max squeaked and she swore she felt their grip shift the bones in her hand.

The ghost – it couldn't be anything but a ghost – disappeared.

It was behind them in an instant, too fast for her to even blink. Shay barely caught the movement out of the corner of her eye. It lunged, one arm that was far too long for any person stretching towards her. It missed Max entirely and grabbed her wrist. The cold cut straight through her hoodie sleeve and down into her bones. The fingers were skeletal, but they were impossibly strong. It yanked her to the side, pulling her hand from Max's grip. She grabbed for them, but missed, her fingers just brushing their sleeve.

"Max!" she screamed. She was pulled towards the mirror. The smooth soles of her canvas shoes scuffed uselessly against the wood floor. She clawed at the bones wrapped around her wrist. It was like trying to grab a handful of ice. Cold jolted up to her elbow. Her fingers tingled with the static of pins and needles.

Her foot hit a box and she fell heavily on her side. The ghost paid no mind, dragging her across the floorboards. She grabbed another box and part of the lid tore away in her hand.

The mirror loomed over her, a hole surrounded by a gilt frame.

It was close, too close.

She swung at the ghost with everything she had. Her fist hit the ghost's sleeve, and it was gone so suddenly that she tumbled back over. It reappeared, instantly, just a few feet away, reaching for her again.

Max shouted something and the ghost sparked green and silver. Parts of him crumbled and faded like an old picture before it vanished.

They grabbed her arm and dragged her to her feet. "C'mon!"

The mist was gathering again, pouring around them, filling the stairwell. Max kicked the door right below the handle. It split, and the second kick broke it completely. They stumbled into the hallway and down the stairs. Shay staggered to the door on trembling legs. The screen door screamed. Shay tripped over the entryway. Max kept her from face planting on the front steps.

The yard was worse in the dark. Max half-dragged her to the sidewalk.

Shay looked back and saw blue light behind the blinds on the second floor. It moved through the house before fizzling away.

"What on earth was that?" Max's voice was much higher than normal.

"That was a ghost," she said it out loud, hardly believing it. If it hadn't touched her, if the cold hadn't sliced right through her, maybe she could have discounted it as an illusion or a hallucination, but her wrist burned. "Let's just go. Please, Max."

"Right." They gave her a worried glance, but didn't let go of her good wrist, leading her to where they'd parked a little ways down the street under a lamppost.

The orange light flickered overhead, but it was better than nothing. Max's old Ford Explorer had never looked so beautiful in any light.

They climbed in and Max started the car, driving a few blocks down before they threw it into park and flopped back against their seat. "I thought we were going to die. I really thought…and my phone! That was proof. That was super proof, right there. A freaking ghost. And he yanked you across the floor! Are you okay?"

"Thank you for that stellar use of priorities." Shay leaned back in her seat and cradled her wrist to her chest. It still hurt. She didn't want to look at it. "Can you turn on the heater?"

"Right, of course." Max cranked the heater on. It had two settings – off and mid-August levels of heat. She would take being slowly roasted alive over the cold that still clung to her.

"I guess we know why they moved."

"Yeah. I guess we do." Max shoved a hand through their hair. At some point the headband they'd been wearing fell out and their dark, thick hair fell over their forehead.

"You look nice like that," Shay told them.

"Okay, now I know you're hurt." They flipped on the dome light. "Let me see."

Shay held out her arm. "What did you do, anyway? To make the ghost disappear. I heard you yell something but…"

"Okay, don't laugh, but I yelled 'begone foul spirit'." Max took her hand with gentle fingers. She didn't laugh. "I figured, y'know, that it couldn't hurt. And then I threw some salt at it. Purifying salt. With lavender. There was lavender in there, too."

Shay stared at them, even as they pulled up her sleeve. She didn't want to see her wrist. "Was it purifying salt or bath stuff?"

"Well, fine, yeah, it's bath stuff. In my defense, it's supposed to be spiritually cleansing," Max said. "I got it at that shop, The Good Cauldron? I figured it'd be good to have, y'know, in case. And it was! It was good. Oh, Shay, this looks bad."

She glanced down and wished she hadn't. Her skin was already mottled with dark purple bruises. Max turned her hand one way, then the other, their touch light and careful but it still hurt. Max's fingers felt like fire against her skin.

"Well, I don't think it's broken," Max said. "And your hands are freezing."

"Yeah." She let them hold both of her hands in theirs. Her hands were tiny in comparison. Most of her was. She didn't even reach five feet in shoes.

"I don't even know what we'd say if we took you to a doctor or a hospital."

"Let's skip that for now," she suggested. "I don't have a lie ready for this. Let's just…see if it goes away on its own?"

"Right, right, okay, I'll wrap it but if it feels worse you tell me and we'll go see someone," Max said. "Maybe Dr. Rahim?"

"Isn't he a vet?" Shay asked. She couldn't remember, exactly, but she was pretty sure that was the name of Max's Nana's vet, who tended to her aging Pomeranian.

"Well, sure, but he went to medical school, and sometimes he, y'know, helps with people stuff. I don't think I'm supposed to tell you that." Max finally let go and Shay immediately missed the warmth.

"Does that make me an honorary Patel, knowing all the family secrets?" Shay asked.

"Sure, O'Brannon, if you want." Max dug the first aid kit out from under their seat. Their car was always immaculate, even if it still smelled a little like pizza on warm days from when they used to do delivery. Their current job was working at a daycare. Shay had seen them in action a few times. They were very good with the kids, always patient and kind, but that wasn't too surprising to her. They'd always been the same way with her.

She decided to not look too deeply into that.

They pulled out an ace bandage and began wrapping her wrist. "Too tight?"

She shook her head. "No."

"Good." They pinned it down and gave her shoulder a pat. "All patched up. I think."

"Are you going to kiss it better with your magic Max powers?"

"Sorry, that ability is reserved for people under the age of five," they said. "You didn't like, hit your head or anything, right?"

"I think I bruised my tailbone," Shay said.

"Definitely not kissing that better."

She snorted. Her entire arm hurt from being yanked around and she was still very, very cold, but she didn't think there was anything Max could do for those things. "And I'm very injured. Spiritually. Metaphysically. Emotionally. The only thing that will heal me now is food. Greasy diner food."

"Yeah?" Max looked amused, at least. And less terrified. "Well, I guess that would be safe. I think I saw one on the way here."

They didn't talk much. Max was pretending that driving took more concentration than it did. Shay didn't mind too much, sinking into her seat and trying not to think of anything at all.

It didn't work very well.

Ghosts were real. She'd been pulled towards a black pit of a mirror by a skeleton in a suit.

"How's your head?" Max asked after driving through another empty intersection. "I have some pain meds. You should eat something before you take them."

"Fine." She hadn't really thought about it, but even the lingering pain was gone. "Completely fine. Must be the adrenaline."

Max glanced at her. "Must be. Well, small mercies, right?"

"Right."

It only took a few minutes to find the place. They parkedin front of a grimy white building with a faded red roof. Curling neon promised "World Famo Apple Pie", the last two letters in "famous" burned out.

Either way, Shay very much doubted the validity of that claim.

Inside it was clear the diner had been built sometime in the seventies, but was obsessed with the fifties. Black and white photos of girls in poodle skirts shared the walls with old records and street signs that had probably never been outside, but had accumulated their own layer of filth. Probably from back when smoking had been allowed in the place. The seats were a worn red vinyl and everything else was neon and chrome. Their waitress, who was wearing a poodle skirt that could have been in one of the photos, dropped off their menus. Shay ordered the apple pie without even looking at it.

"Dessert before food?" Max's eyebrows rose. They'd found a spare headband in their car and fixed themself up to be somewhat presentable by their standards, and a sparkling beacon one could only hope to aspire to by Shay's much lower standards. She hadn't even bothered to try and tame her half un-done braid.

"It's world famo, Max. Obviously I have to try it."

They shrugged. "I mean if it's world famo then I suppose you gotta. So um. Just gonna, shoot the elephant in the room. I'm sorry."

"For what?" Shay was surprised. "You haven't even gloated yet."

"For, y'know. All that." Max gestured in a vague way. "I thought it'd be normal, you know? A few creaks, I'd get scared, you'd laugh, we'd go home and watch a stupid movie."

"Typical Friday night stuff," she said. She sighed, her shoulders slumping. "I'm sorry, too. For laughing at you. Because apparently ghosts are real, I guess, and they're thriving in…Doveton, Idaho, of all places. Oh, man, do you think that the creaking sounds on my parents' stairs is a ghost? Is it just… creeping on me every time I visit? This opens up more questions than it answers and I don't think I like it."

She talked because there wasn't much else she could do. The diner felt like a completely different reality than the attic. She was having trouble meshing the black and white tile with the hard wood and mist.

"I mean we could check it out…"

"Really?" Shay looked at them incredulously. "After all that you still want to go ghost hunting?"

"Well. I dunno." Max stared at the menu, clearly not seeing it. "Ghosts are real! They're real, Shay, I was right. And actually that's scary, but I didn't get to record it because it killed my phone. So…"

"Don't even joke about going back," Shay said. "Not even a little."

"I wasn't going to." Max held up their hands defensively. "Besides, there's no guarantees that the murder ghost would show up again. Sometimes ghosts don't show up for years, and even though it sucked our equipment dry, it must have used up so much energy."

The waitress chose that exact moment to set the pie down in front of Shay, along with two mugs of coffee. They both looked up at her, frozen. It was probably very funny, but if the waitress thought so it didn't show on her face.

"DnD," Max said, like it explained everything.

"Are you ready to order?" She clearly didn't care if they were talking about tabletop RPGs or planning their next homicide. Shay hadn't even looked at the menu but figured french toast was always a safe bet. Max ordered a burger and fries and handed both menus back to her with a smile that wasn't returned.

"Don't judge," they told Shay.

"Have I ever?" she asked, pulling the pie a little closer. "If it makes you feel better, I'll have some of your fries."

"Heck no, they're my fries. Mine."

"Chill, I'll leave your fries alone." It was a little awkward maneuvering her fork with her left hand, but she managed to take a bite of the pie. It probably had apples and was pie shaped. That was the best she could think of it. Max took a bite, too, and made a face. "Oh, it's not that bad."

"I think it might be world famo for being the worst," Max said.

"Gotta be famo for something," Shay said. Max took another bite despite their face. "If it's so bad why are you eating it?"

"Because I'm buying it, obviously," Max said. "And don't protest, because I almost got you killed by a murder ghost. And you're broke."

"I can't argue with that."

They took a swig of their coffee as if to seal the deal, made a face, and added enough cream and sugar it turned a murky gray.

Shay cut another bite of pie but just spread dubiously caramelized apples over her plate. Maybe the diner had been a bad idea. It was too cold, the windows were big and dark, and everyone there was probably twenty years older than them. The music being pumped over the speakers was extremely country and almost too tinny to hear the twangs. Everything felt bleak, tired, and some level of dirty.

"That thing can't follow us, right?" She curled her arm up to her chest.

"Even if it's still around. It seemed pretty site-bound to the mirror, but if it makes you feel better, we'll stay at my place tonight," Max said. "I warded my place against ghosts. I mean, I did like, a ritual thing? With a candle? And like, lavender? I found it online."

"Oh, well, if you found it online."

"Shush, you, or I'll really lay on the gloating. Anyway, it should be safe. I'd ward your place but I don't think that your brother would appreciate me burning herbs."

"Don't worry, Duncan probably already burns enough herbs to keep us safe." Shay smiled, a little.

"I mean, I guess." Max smiled back.

"Besides, ghosts can't enter our apartment, the price of our rent repels them," Shay said. "But yeah, I figured that was the plan. There's no way I'm letting you out of my sight for at least thirty-six hours to a year or so."

"That's a pretty broad window of time."

"I like to keep my options open," Shay said. "We're going to need so much junk food. And movies. Really bad movies. Like the absolute worst."

She didn't want to be left alone to her thoughts for any amount of time.

"Wow, you're going to get the most out of that thirty-six hours, huh?"

"To a year. You could say I'm planning to use them…to the max." She grinned when Max groaned. "Okay, yeah, that one was bad. I apologize."

"They're all bad, you should apologize for all of them."

"The only thing I should apologize for is this diner," Shay said. "Let's not ever come here again."

She said it like it wasn't the first time they'd been there, but she supposed going to one diner failing miserably to bring back some long-lost aesthetic was pretty much like going to them all.

"Deal."

Chapter 4:

Mothman is Real (And Believes in You)

The parking lot was close enough to the freeway that Shay could still hear the traffic, but otherwise the night was silent, cold and clear. The light dimmed the stars to mere pinpricks.

The french toast and the four fries she'd managed to snag sat like a lump in her stomach. She hadn't been able to eat more of the pie.

"World famo, sure." Max glared at the sign. "World famo for being terrible."

They kept muttering about it as they unlocked their car. Shay tried hard not to smile but she failed, climbing into the front seat. "Are you done?"

"Tasted like it was from the frozen aisle but worse. Now I'm done," Max said. They pulled their phone up from where they'd started charging it with an external battery between the seats. "Oh, good. It lives. Let's see…"

They pulled up the video. Max slid to the end. The camera approached the attic door. There was a flash of light she hadn't noticed before, streaming into the hallway as she opened the door. The screen jittered and went dark.

"Well. That sucks." Max tucked their phone back into the center console. "Guess I can post an account, but it doesn't really do much without proof, y'know?"

Shay wiggled deeper into the seat. "Yeah, but even if you posted a video people would say it was fake. Photoshop or something."

"True. I'll analyze the rest of the video and stuff later, see if we caught anything."

"Sounds good," Shay said. "Hey, I have a question."

"I might have an answer."

"Is Mothman real?"

Max laughed and she elbowed them. "Ow! Sorry, it was just… really?"

"Well, ghosts are real." Shay ducked her head to hide that she was blushing. "So. Mothman could be real. Maybe."

"I mean, anything is possible, I guess." Max started the car with a rumble like thunder. "Wait, we have to do this right. With a scale of real to not real. Ghosts, definitely real. Mothman? Real in my heart."

"Wow," Shay said.

"Hey, you started this discussion," Max reminded her, adjusting a few of the vents so they pointed at Shay. "We'll come back to him. Bigfoot."

"Sure," Shay said. "Why not. Just a big fuzzy guy living in Washington. I know like, five people that fit that description."

"I bet you do," Max grinned. "Aliens."

"Real, but they've never visited Earth."

Max nodded. "El Chupacabra?"

"Coyote with mange."

"Ooh, nice answer." Max plugged in her phone for her. She was sure no one had even tried to contact her. Max was the only person who texted her regularly, and even they knew that her answering was hit or miss. "Werewolves."

"Does that count as a cryptid?" Shay asked. "I don't know. Sure. Werewolves."

"Fresno Night Crawlers."

"Those are weird," Shay admitted. She'd watched the video with Max a few times. "Inconclusive."

"There's literally video evidence-"

"Inconclusive!" she repeated.

"Fine, I'll give you that," Max said. "How's your wrist? Any better?"

"A little." Shay lifted her hand, rotating it slowly. "No grating sounds or stabbing pain, so I'm probably fine."

Even the cold was fading away, but that might have been because of all of the hot air blasting at her, from the vents and her best friend.

"Well… that's good," Max said. "Still, if it gets worse, let me know."

They pulled out of the parking lot with a questionable rattle, but neither of them commented on it.

"I will," Shay said. "Sorry about your footage."

"It's fine, I'm sure I got something," Max said. "What matters is we saw a ghost. A real ghost! Not just a shadow or…or an impression or a voice. It was a fully formed apparition!"

"Yeah I think I prefer the shadows," Shay said.

"What do you think that mirror was doing in there?" Max spoke like they'd bottled up everything and had given it all a really good shake before opening up. "Do you think it was tied to it? There's a lot of superstition about mirrors and death, do you think maybe that's true?"

"Well, I thought it didn't really match their décor," Shay said. "A little too IKEA showroom to be side by side with a scary antique mirror. Then I was a little too busy being dragged across the floor."

"Yeah." Max had the decency to sound a little subdued. "What really matters is that you're okay."

"Thanks, I'm okay." Shay patted their shoulder. "So local family buys or inherits a mirror. Mirror has ghost. Family moves away. We really Scooby-ed that one."

"Us meddling kids and all that. I wonder where the mirror came from, then," Max said.

"Probably some antique store." Shay shrugged. "They probably didn't have a sign like, 'this mirror is super haunted, buy at your own risk'."

"I'll see what I can dig up," Max said. "The other question is, where was it dragging you?"

"Into the mirror," Shay said. "To be its bride. No thanks, by the way. I'm not marrying a ghost. That's a dead end relationship."

"I could leave you here," Max warned.

"You won't," she countered.

They sighed. "I won't."

They turned off the highway into the pass. Her brother always drove over the hills from Doveton into Teton Falls, but Max insisted the canyon was faster. It was also narrow, incredibly dark, and full of trees that looked like they were reaching down to grab unwary cars trundling by.

It was probably the quickest route when it came to miles, but since Max had to slow down or risk getting bludgeoned by some big fancy truck whipping around a corner, Shay was pretty sure it was slower.

"Would you mind being on the show?" Max asked.

"I'm already on your show," Shay reminded them.

"I mean like, an official interview."

"What, like 'I was attacked by ghosts and survived! Hear the terrifying details of my near abduction!'"

Max laughed. "Sure, something like that. So. Would you?"

"Yeah, sure," Shay agreed. "Loch Ness Monster."

"Why not, it's a big lake," Max said.

"I don't think our method of deciding what's real or not is very scientific."

Max shrugged. "Who said it has to be scientific? Sometimes it's about how you feel. Loveland frog?"

"What on earth is the Loveland frog?" Shay asked.

"Big humanoid frog in Ohio," Max explained.

"You know what, sure, it's Ohio, there's probably a big humanoid frog there," she said. She knew Max was just distracting her, but she was grateful for it. "Flatwoods Monster."

"Honestly, on the fence about it," Max said. "Okay, back to Mothman."

"Not real," she said.

"Seriously?" Max laughed. "You're giving the Loveland frog a pass but not Mothman?"

"I think his legend is overexaggerated," Shay said. "Besides, he foretells disaster or whatever, right? I don't believe in clairvoyance or whatever. Prophecies. Any of that seeing the future stuff."

"You might not believe in Mothman, but he believes in you." Max glanced over to grin at her.

She rolled her eyes. "Yeah, okay."

"Be the person Mothman knows you can be eventually."

"You know, maybe you should—watch out!"

Someone stood on the road. Shay had the impression of long hair and a skirt before Max swerved and she was tossed into the door despite her seatbelt.

Max slammed on the brakes and pulled onto the side of the road with a crunch of gravel. Dust wafted up into the beams of the headlights.

"I don't think I hit anyone." They were already undoing their seatbelt. "You saw someone, right?"

"Are you sure?" her voice had gone almost squeaky. She hopped out of the car after them. The canyon behind the car was awash with the red from the taillights. She couldn't see anyone on the road.

"Hello?" Max called. "Are you okay? Did your car break down?"

"Max…" Shay realized a moment too late they'd broken the cardinal rule of horror movies.

They'd left the car.

It was already a cold night.

The temperature dived to freezing in moments, her breath pluming in front of her and frost creeping across the pavement.

Something glowed to her left. She was almost too afraid to look.

The woman on the road – it must have been her – was standing next to her. She was the same blue as the ghost in the attic. Her hair was floating like she was underwater, skirt swirling around her legs.

The woman rotated to face her. Her feet weren't touching the ground.

She didn't have a face, just black static where it should have been.

Shay screamed. She ran back to the car, slamming the door shut. Max was climbing in with her, closing the front door. "What happened? Are you okay?"

"Just go!" She smacked their arm like it would get them to move faster.

"Put on your seatbelt!"

"Max!"

Something in her voice got through to them. They put the car into drive, tearing away from the shoulder and back onto the road. Shay twisted around. The woman was standing in the middle of the road again.

She vanished before they made the next turn.

"Ugh." She flopped back against the seat, barely remembering to yank the seatbelt around her again.

"What was that all about?" Max asked.

"Obviously No Face Lady standing in the middle of the road?" Shay stared at them. "Ghost. Must have been a ghost. She was so cold. And, I repeat, she had no face."

She wrapped her arms around herself in an attempt to feel safe. It didn't help.

"Shay, I didn't see anything," Max sounded worried.

"How could you not see anything?" she gestured wildly to them. "It was right there! Right next to me. Glowing! Just like Jack Skellington in the attic!"

"Just like… wait, what?" Max glanced at her, clearly trying to check on her and watch the road at the same time. "Jack Skellington?"

"Tall, skeleton, vaudeville suit. I mean, I think it was, anyway," Shay said. "Okay, with the pinstripes it was kind of on the nose, but I am hilarious and right."

"That's debatable," Max said. "You saw a skeleton?"

"With a top hat. And a monocle." She felt those were very important details. "…Why? What did you see?"

"A tall, dark shape with glowing red eyes," Max said.

"You said full apparition."

"That is a full apparition, it looked like a 3D shadow," Max said. "It went right through me, and it was super cold, but it could grab you? And then you saw…I don't know, a road ghost? Shay, I think…I think you're seeing more than I am because you're special. You have like, the sight, or something."

"You know the only sight I have is bad," Shay said. She could barely see anything when she took her glasses off.

"No, I mean like, ghost sight," Max said. "You can see ghosts."

Shay had no idea how to respond to that. Dead was dead. Her mom said reincarnation, her dad said heaven or hell. She figured there wasn't much room for restless spirits, either way.

"Shay?" Max asked.

"That's dumb," she said. She kicked her feet up so they were against the dashboard. "Ghosts? That's dumb. That's so dumb."

"That's not safe-"

"Max, your airbags don't work." Shay had seen the notices to get them fixed on Max's desk on more than one occasion. "Riding in your car is already fundamentally unsafe. Just let me have this."

"I can do that," Max said. "Are you okay?"

"No! Of course I'm not okay!" Shay said. "I thought, well, I just thought that we finally went to the first actually haunted place, but now you're telling me that…and since ghosts are real, how can that be the first haunted place we went to? We went to a prison! And a murder barn!"

"Well, like I said, the murder wasn't actually confirmed—"

"An owl tried to steal your eyes, Max, it was a murder barn," Shay said. She sighed and thunked her head against the seat. They'd left the pass and were driving past the larger houses built outside of town. Lit windows twinkled like fireflies at the end of long driveways. "It just doesn't make any sense. Why now? I've never seen a ghost before. If I have the sight, or whatever you think I have, it…it just doesn't make any sense."

"I could be wrong," Max said. "It was just a suggestion. Throwing things out there. Maybe it wasn't even a ghost. Maybe it was…I don't know, a gas leak. Or electrical wires

causing a frequency, or something. That happens, you know. Maybe ghosts aren't real after all. Right?"

"You don't believe that."

Max shrugged. "Sleepover. We can figure it out tonight, or tomorrow. You can stay as long as you need."

They reached over and patted her knee reassuringly.

"You can't stop believing in ghosts on me," Shay said. "What would Mothman say?"

"Mothman just wants you to be okay," Max said.

Shay nodded, not sure what else could be said. The cold was gone, even from her wrist. All that was left was a deep ache.

CHAPTER 5:
DUNCAN DONUTS

"Hey, dorks, did you catch Bigfoot?"

Shay whipped out her phone and took a picture of her brother. "Now we have. Wow. Uglier than anyone ever could have imagined."

"This is going to change the world of cryptozoology forever," Max agreed. "You were right, Shay, he is real."

"I knew it."

"Oh, ha ha. Ha." Duncan flipped them both off.

She had caught him in his rattiest sweats with more food than he could possibly need. Despite his atrocious eating habits, her and Duncan were opposites when it came to shape. She was short and chubby. He was nearly as tall as Max and wiry. He looked a lot like their mom, she supposed she took more after their dad.

"Here Bigfoot is in his natural habitat, the couch," she did her best, or worst, impression of a nature documentary voice over. "With no natural predators, or potential mates, it spends all of its quality time in front of the tv watching bad anime."

"Wow, sick burn, nerd." Duncan rolled his eyes. "You kids having a sleepover?"

"Yeah, but at Max's, away from your grossness." Shay set the new photo as Duncan's contact picture. "And for the record, we were ghost hunting."

"Who ya gonna call," Duncan said. "Hey, speaking of, I have a favor to ask."

Shay sat down on the ottoman so Max could have the slightly more comfortable leather chair. Becky, their cat, rubbed against her ankles and she scratched her head. "Have a funny way of asking for favors, how many times did you insult us?"

"Four, if you include him calling us kids," Max said.

"You guys are kids," Duncan said. "So that doesn't count. Besides, this is right up your little nerd alley. Yeah, yeah, technically six insults, I can count too, Maximus."

"That's not what it's short for," Max muttered.

"Maxwell. Maximum Overdrive. Maxcellenté."

Admittedly Shay had never told him that Max wasn't short for anything at all, but she doubted that would keep Duncan from giving increasingly bad guesses. "Just spit it out, Donuts."

"Right, right, so the library is doing this big Halloween thing with one of the local groups, and - this is super cool you guys will love it- it's a ghost hunt." Duncan grinned at them. "You know that old theater on Becker? The one with the columns? We got permission to set up in there, how rad is that?"

"Why aren't you set up in the library if it's…for the library?" Max asked. "It's supposed to be haunted."

"That's what I said, but they said something about it being bad for business," Duncan shrugged. "Anyway, what do you say? A real old building, actual ghost hunters, it's going to be amazing."

"We're already actual ghost hunters," Max muttered.

Shay was aware of the building. She'd gone to a play for school once, before it shut down. It had been terrible, but the local acting scene in Teton Falls wasn't exactly an overflowing well of talent. If Duncan had asked her to go into the old theater with a bunch of geeks to look for spirits just a few hours earlier, she would have agreed in a heartbeat. As it was, she wasn't sure she ever wanted to think about ghost hunting again. "I dunno, Dunc."

"Oh, c'mon! You love ghost hunting. You were literally just ghost hunting," Duncan reminded her. "This is your chance to go to like, the coolest building in the city with real equipment. No insults to Max's phone."

"It is a cool old building," Max said. "Is the group P.E.I.R.S.?"

"That's the one." Duncan snapped his fingers and pointed at Max. "Not surprised you already know who they are. Anyway, we just need a few extra hands. I won't even make you be in the video because I'm that much of a kind and generous soul. You get free pizza, and one of the ghost hunting guys? Super hot. Met him at that Pride thing and we've been talking. Off and on. So, after we pair off I wouldn't mind, y'know, getting a little scared. Holding his hand. I don't ask for much, really."

"Ugh, the full truth comes out." Shay sighed. "I'm your wingman."

"Wingperson," Max said.

"We're winging it, for sure." Duncan nodded. "Please? Pretty pretty please? I'll do dishes, for like, a week. And free pizza. And you get to work with real actual live ghost hunters. Well, for Teton Falls, anyway. I shouldn't even have to beg. You guys should be over the moon for this."

Shay thought about the skeleton, coming through the mirror. What if something like that happened to Duncan? Or their group? Max had been able to fend off the ghost, if the worst occurred it would be better if they were there to help. She looked at Max and either they were thinking the same thing, or they did want to meet the people from P.E.I.R.S. "Yeah, fine. When is it?"

"Yes! I knew you'd want to! And it's a good thing you agreed on your own. I already signed you guys up." Duncan grinned at her. "Tomorrow night! You need to be there by five. Thanks, ShayShay, you're the best. I wuv you."

"Gross," Shay said.

"Seriously?" Max asked. "You put off telling us until now?"

"I put the pan in panic." Duncan gave them finger guns and Max groaned. "Hey, that one was pretty good, you shut up."

"Shay, I'm going to pack up your crap." Max left the chair and headed down the hallway.

"Yeah, don't worry, I'll just be…bi myself." Shay grinned when she heard Max groan even louder. She got to her feet.

"And all aces," Duncan added.

"Nice." Shay nodded. "Enjoy your garbage entertainment."

"Oh, I will. I absolutely will," Duncan said. "I'll text you the deets. And Shay, don't be a turd to Max. They're a good…is dude out this week or…?"

Shay gave him a withering look. "It's out forever as far as you're concerned."

"Okie doke. Person, then. A great person. Striving for non-turdness is the takeaway message here."

"You're a turd," Shay said.

"Wow. That was an incredible comeback. Super witty. Completely blew my mind." Duncan raised his soda to her. "Anyway, have fun making out or whatever."

"We do not-"

"I said whatever, can't hold that against me." Duncan shrugged and started up his show again. Brightly colored anime people started hitting each other while yelling. A lot.

Shay was pretty sure they'd already seen this one, but she wasn't going to question it. When she got back to her room Max had already picked her laundry off of the floor and packed her old duffle bag for her. "Hey."

"I'd be embarrassed, but honestly you've seen my room in worse states," Shay said. "Thanks, Max."

"No problem. Just grab your toiletries and we can go." They looked up at her. "You good?"

"I…" She decided she didn't really want to relay the conversation she'd just had to them. Partly because it contained the word "turd". Multiple times. "Yeah. I'm great. You're awesome."

"Obviously." Max beamed at her.

She snagged the few things from the bathroom she needed, shoving them on top of the carefully folded clothes. Max had packed enough for a few nights. They snagged the bag before she could even try to carry it. "Oh, c'mon. I'm fine."

"I know," Max said. They headed out, saying a final goodbye to Duncan who waved at them with half of a burrito.

Max insisted they did not need a snack run, which Shay was grateful for. She was more tired than she realized, dealing with Duncan had pretty much finished wiping her out. She leaned against the window and watched the pools of light from the streetlamps rush by. Max didn't say anything. She didn't mind.

The apartment Max lived in was in their Nana's basement. It was big and painted white to make it seem brighter despite the small, recessed windows. There was a little kitchenette, too. Sometimes she heard their parents or their Nana walk around upstairs, but for the most part they let them do whatever they wanted with only the occasional text reminding them of the late hour and their volume.

Shay flopped down on the couch. It was remarkably hideous under the blankets covering it – it had been a hand-me-down from upstairs — but it was comfortable. "Sorry you got roped into…all of that."

"Oh, it's fine." Max pulled a box of microwavable popcorn from the cupboard. "P.E.I.R.S. is a really cool group. Stands for Paranormal Eastern Idaho Research Society, in case you wanted to know. They seem pretty cool. And hey, we can test my theory way earlier than I thought we would in a relatively safe environment."

"Your theory?" Shay asked.

"About you, and…all of that," Max said. "But popcorn first. You look like you need it."

"Aww Max, you're the best." Shay shrugged out of her hoodie. Underneath she was wearing a garage band t-shirt that she realized belonged to Duncan, but if he wanted to keep all of his clothes then he would just have to do the laundry sometimes.

She couldn't complain too much, since he was letting her crash in the spare room for free.

She started to unwind the bandage on her wrist, but Max made distressed noises. "Not until I'm over there!"

"Is it part of your popcorn worthy theory?" Shay stopped what she was doing.

"No. Well, maybe." Max pulled out a bowl. The popping sounded a little like all she remembered of the garage band's music. "Maybe not. You still have to wait."

"Fine." Shay flopped back against the cushions. She felt comfortably tired, like the world had taken on a soft glow. That might have been Max's distaste for overhead lights — their living room was lit by a handful of lamps and a string of fairy lights around the window.

It was a safe and quiet flavor of exhaustion.

Max sat down next to her, the popcorn bowl on the coffee table and two ginger ales had appeared out of nowhere.

"Okay. Popcorn popped. Let's see that wrist."

"It doesn't really hurt anymore." Shay held her hand out to them. Despite what she said, Max was very careful while unwrapping the bandage. Once it was off, they let out a hiss of breath between their teeth.

She could see why. Her entire wrist was purple, a mottled bruise in the shape of fingers curling around it. It didn't hurt like a bruise should have. She thought seeing it would make the pain flare up again, but it stayed dull.

"It's not as bad as it looks."

"Good, because it looks really bad." Max touched the bruises with fingers so gentle she barely felt them. "You're not cold anymore, so that's good. Actually…"

They felt her forehead with their free hand.

"That's high tech."

Max ignored her. "I think you have a fever. A little one."

"Oh, well, as long as it's just a little one." Shay leaned against their shoulder. "You're warm."

"Because you feel cold. Because you have a fever." Max pulled the blanket off the back of the couch and wrapped it around both of them, anyway. "Do you want me to bandage it back up? Or…get a brace, maybe?"

"I think I'm good." Shay shrugged. "It just looks gross. Maybe it's because it was a ghost? Weird."

"Could be," Max said. "I guess all we can do is monitor it."

"Guess so." Shay snagged a handful of popcorn. "Mm burny. You really know the way to a girl's heart."

"Oh yeah. That's me. Plans, burned popcorn, ghost hunting. I'm smooth." Max grinned at her. "Like butter."

"Yeah, you're a flawless being, we all know. When do I get my theories? I'm dying here." Shay paused for a moment. "Maybe literally, and that's why I'm seeing ghosts now. You could be a ghost."

"Is Duncan a ghost, too?" Max was no longer grinning.

"He's haunting the apartment," Shay said. "Maybe that's why he always seems to be there."

"He goes to work, Shay."

"To the library! He could be haunting the library, too," Shay said. "I don't go to work. I could be a ghost."

"Well, you're not, and that was not one of my theories." Max leaned forward to pull their laptop out from under the couch. "Okay, settle in."

Shay leaned against them again and gave them a thumbs up. "I am settled. So hard."

Max opened their laptop and started poking around in the files. Shay was pretty sure she'd been on most of the ghost hunt folders, even the one they eventually opened. They pulled up a photo. It was in a cave, and she remembered being in there. Supposedly it had been haunted by a horse thief, but she couldn't remember the details of the story. Something about getting cornered in the cave and shot by the local authorities.

"So, first off, before theories, I want to test something, so…right here." They hovered their mouse over a gap in the rocks, highlighted to daylight brightness the cave probably never saw by the camera's flash. "What do you see?"

Chapter 6: Ghost Eyes

"Not even this one?"

Shay looked very carefully at the picture. It was the murder barn, or at least she was pretty sure it was. All abandoned barns looked the same after a while. Empty rafters and a loft. "Nope."

"Hm." Max pouted at the screen. "Wait! What about without your glasses?"

"I guess." Shay shoved her glasses up into her hair before leaning forward to squint at the screen. "Oh, wow, it is different."

"Really?"

"Yeah. It's blurry."

"Oh." Max hooked their phone up to the laptop. "Let me upload the pictures from tonight and see if you see anything there."

Shay knocked her glasses back down. They fell off and she had to scramble to put them back on her face, shoving her hair back. "You didn't check any of them?"

"Didn't really get a chance to," Max admitted. "Hopefully I got something."

"Or nothing." Shay really hoped they hadn't caught an image of the ghost, however it would be interpreted by a camera lens.

"You don't have to, if you don't want to," Max said, too quickly. "I mean, that was probably…okay, it was definitely traumatizing. And it wasn't that long ago. And it's fine. Really. Nevermind. We'll do that later. Or never!"

"Max, it's fine." She patted their arm. "I'm not that fragile. Probably. Besides, only confirmed ghost house, so…I get it. The other places might not have been haunted at all. This is for science. More sciency science."

"True." Max nodded. "I mean, it might be that you're seeing what the camera sees, which means none of this really matters. In fact, I'm pretty sure that's it, but…woah."

"What?" Shay looked at the computer. It had loaded all of Max's pictures, and they all looked very different than what she expected.

They were too dark, some of them completely black. Streaks of pale blue floated through the house, smeared like smoke. The shots taken upstairs were worse, the shadows almost looked like people, the lines were bright and tangled all together, converging on the attic door like the center of a spiderweb.

"Weird exposure?" Shay suggested, even as it felt like something cold was crawling up her spine.

"I would normally count that as a reason, but I took these with my phone," Max reminded her. "It's never done anything like that before."

"Wait. I thought of something." She pulled up one of the many realtor websites and punched in the address. She found the house and scrolled through the pictures. "Found it. Check this out."

The pictures of the outside looked relatively normal. There were only pictures of the bottom floor and the basement for the inside. They were all the same as Max's pictures. The realtor apologized for the exposure and promised pictures of the upstairs were coming soon.

"It was the mirror," Max said, sliding through more photos. "We have definitely Scooby-ed that."

"Meddling kids the heck out of it," Shay agreed. "So we can definitely figure out my weird… ghost brain thing. What if it is just a brain thing? Like, there was something there and my eyes were just like 'probs a skeleton in a suit'. I mean with those headaches…"

That sent a pulse of nervousness through her chest.

"I'll put that in the maybe pile," Max said. "You said you didn't have a headache. Did it come back?"

She wiggled her head from side to side experimentally. The ache that had lodged itself behind her eyes had dissipated entirely. It should have been a relief, but it just felt strange. She'd had a headache for so long that the absence felt almost wrong. "Nope."

"Well…good." Max nodded. They frowned. "Even if it was a…brain thing, I saw it, too. And what about the woman on the road?"

"I probably imagined that, because of the trauma," Shay said.

"You saw a full-blown apparition," Max said. "And I don't think you imagined it. I didn't see anything, but it was way too cold out there."

"I never want to hear the word 'apparition' again," Shay said.

Max nodded. "Okay, yeah, that's fair. Still, clearly something is going on with you. Whether it's the sight or…"

"Please don't call it that." Shay rubbed at her temple. "You must be super jealous, I bet you'd love to have 'the sight' or whatever."

"I dunno. Maybe?" Max shrugged. "Mostly…I just want you to be okay."

Shay felt like the jerk she had been. "Okay, yeah, I get that. Sorry, I'm being a butt."

"You're entitled to one free night of butt-ness." Max smiled a bit.

"Aww thanks."

"I guess we're going to need new hobbies," Max said.

"Yeah, I guess, since we'll have to avoid haunted places," Shay said. "Let's brainstorm our new and far less haunted life goals."

"Hm well. More bad tv?" Max asked.

"Actually, I'm thinking… Ghost Eyes. Vigilante for Justice." Shay gave them finger guns. "Pew pew."

Max's expression went from tentatively curious to flat. "Okay. All right. Ten points for the name, I'll give you that. Minus a million points for assuming we'd even need vigilante justice in Teton Falls."

"Not like seeing ghosts is much of a super power," Shay admitted, slumping back into the couch. "'Villain! Please take three steps to the left so you can feel a chill and maybe a side helping of existential dread! Ha! You are defeated!' Yeah, okay, that's not going to work."

"Again, that's only if there were villains anywhere near here," Max reminded her. "Which there aren't, because this is a town of twenty-thousand people. Tops."

"Okay, first off, I went off to college and I can assure you it's boring everywhere," Shay said.

"You were in Moscow," Max said. The "cow" made it obvious it was the small town in western Idaho. "It's smaller than here."

"Five thousand people bigger and still no more hopping than this place is," Shay said. "Second, because I wasn't done with my list before you so rudely interrupted me, I am here so it is exciting.”

“I’ll give you that one,” Max said. “Third?”

“Third, we got attacked like… right near here. Hours ago.”

“I mean, okay, fair, but that was in Doveton,” Max said. “But point made. Maybe you could be like, a ghost hunting vigilante. Help people like that family before they have to run away.”

“Ghost Eyes, Vigilante of Ghost Justice.”

“We’ll work on the name.”

“You gave me ten points.”

“And yet, I could have given so many more.”

Shay stared up at the ceiling for a few moments, letting the silence settle between them. Someone walked across the floor above them. It was probably Max’s dad, judging by how heavy the steps were, but their Nana somehow still managed to stomp everywhere.

It was a few minutes before she spoke again. “Any other theories?”

“Just that…I dunno, maybe the entity-”

“Jack.”

“Yes, fine, maybe Jack was what jump started your uh…ghost eyes,” they said. “It seemed pretty strong.”

“It did haul us both across the floor.” She rubbed her wrist at the memory.

“I mean, y’know, in a ghost way.” Max tugged a hand through their hair. Their headband landed on the cushion next to them, dark hair flopping around their face. “An encounter with a strong entity could potentially trigger any latent psychic abilities you might have.”

“Wow, that sounded all good and scientific, I was on board, and then you had to go with ‘latent psychic abilities’?” Shay rolled her eyes. “Do I look like Professor X to you?”

"Not even remotely," Max said without missing a beat. "Psychic doesn't just mean reading minds or lifting objects with your thoughts-"

"Though that would be rad."

"Extremely. But it also means any sort of extrasensory perception. Or ESP," Max said.

"Seriously?" Shay asked. "I don't care for that. I'm no psychic."

"I mean, the headaches…"

"Are probably unrelated," Shay said.

"Really, what are the odds that you have headaches that mysteriously disappear when you see your first ghost?" Max sighed. "Sorry. That came out meaner than I intended. I'm just saying that it's a possibility. We don't have to call it that. How about, you saw a ghost, and your magic powers activated."

"I guess," Shay said. "But Dunc says the headaches run in the family. He gets them all the time, too."

"Maybe he needs to see a ghost, too?" Max suggested. "Maybe we'll find out tomorrow?"

"Please don't joke about that," Shay said. "I should have said no. I've had enough ghosts."

But that was the entire reason she'd agreed. She was afraid of that exact thing happening.

"Sorry." Max got up off of the couch, snagging their headband as they went. "I'm gonna take out my contacts, you need anything?"

"Just you." Shay batted her eyes at them.

Max grinned in return. "Of course, but I meant more in the line of chocolate."

"Oh Max, you do love me."

Max laughed. "Sometimes. I'll be right back."

"Sometimes! I am always a delight." She flopped down on the couch properly, snagging a throw pillow and tucking it behind her head, staring at Max's ancient bubble screened tv.

Thinking really hard at it did not magically turn it on.

If psychic powers were real they could at least have the good sense to be useful.

She closed her eyes and the skeleton flooded back into her vision, bony fingers reaching for her.

A loud scratching noise startled her.

Max wasn't in the room.

The scratching noise again. She slid into the back of the couch, pulling the blanket over her head slowly and carefully.

It didn't help, the sound continued.

Max once told her that the desk in their apartment used to belong to their grandfather. He'd died, long before Max was born, but he used to write at the desk. Now it was just a place where Max's mail and keys were tossed.

There was a pause in the scratching and a creak of someone shifting.

She was almost relieved when it started up again.

Max had told her that their Nana would sometimes hear writing from the desk. One time she'd seen her husband sitting there and immediately moved it downstairs. Max tried to record the noise, more than once, but they said they'd never heard anything.

She was frozen, hiding under a throw blanket. She didn't want to sit up and see Max's dead grandpa. What if he turned violent, like the other ghost? Even if he didn't, she would still be seeing her best friend's grandparent they'd never had a chance to meet. That felt like crossing a line.

And if he was sitting there, if she could see him, she didn't know what she would do.

The chair shifted again and someone stood up. Heavy footfalls approached the couch, the air growing colder. She could see the glow through the holes in the blanket, even as she tried desperately not to look, but she was more afraid to close her eyes.

The bathroom door opened and the presence vanished, like it had never been there. The room grew warmer and the heaviness of the air lifted.

"One chocolate bar, your grace. Why are you under the blanket?"

Shay sat up and hoped she didn't look like as much of a crazed, wide-eyed lunatic as she felt. "It's comforting. And comfortable. Yay, chocolate."

"Are you okay?" Max sat down next to her again. "That was a dumb question."

"Nah, it wasn't. I'm okay." Shay knew she shouldn't feel guilty, she hadn't asked for Max's dead relative to come into the room the second they left, but she did anyway. "If I have this…ability. Let's call it that. Anyway, shouldn't I be seeing ghosts everywhere? All the time? I mean, there has to be billions and billions of dead people. So many dead people. And that's just like, the colonists. Think of the people who lived here originally? That's so many ghosts. So many angry ghosts. I'd be pissed. Pissed as hell."

"Well, okay, we have to assume that not everyone leaves a ghost," Max said. "And you might not be seeing on all…well. Frequencies isn't quite the right word, but it's going to have to do. I mean, ghosts are basically the energy and memories that someone leaves behind when they die, so anyone who dies peacefully in their sleep is probably not leaving behind a lot of energy."

"I guess that makes sense," Shay said. "Maybe there's something about it in your forums. I can't be the only person with a whacked out ghost frequency."

"That's not a bad idea." Max nodded.

"And maybe Nana knows something!" Shay said. Max's grandma insisted that she call her Nana, too. "She's always telling you not to go on those ghost hunts, and she's always talking about, what are they called, voots?"

"Bhoot," Max corrected her on the pronunciation. "Most of her information comes from dramas, so I'm not sure how much that helps. She's just afraid I'm going to get possessed."

"Is that a thing that can happen?" Shay poked them. "Are you possessed right now? Maybe I'm possessed."

"I think you'd probably know," Max said.

"Possessed with knowledge that you're a big ghost nerd."

They rolled their eyes. "You're not possessed. And neither am I. That's why she gave me this."

They hooked their thumb on a chain around their neck and showed her the necklace they were wearing. It was just a double horseshoe. She'd been expecting something more elaborate, but it was cute, in its own way.

"I didn't know you liked horses this much," Shay said.

Max sighed. "It's a symbol that guards against bad stuff. Like demons. And it's iron. It keeps me safe."

"Oh." Shay still thought they probably liked horses more than they were telling her. "Guess I need one of those."

"Sure, I'll get you one," they promised. "In the meantime, I'll sift through people being, well, kind of weird about ghosts. You can get some rest. I don't think I'm ever going to sleep again."

"You're not going to leave me out here, right?" Shay asked. It felt kind of dumb, Max's bedroom was literally off the living room, but she was afraid the moment they left the scratching would start up again.

"Nah, of course not," Max said. "Eat that chocolate and we'll get the couch bed pulled out."

"Okay." She didn't really want the chocolate. It felt like she was running on fumes, trying to reach some imaginary finish line. "Hey, Max, um. I'm sorry. That I didn't believe you. And sorry I didn't say sorry before. Just. Sorry."

"You already apologized. Don't worry about it, you still went ghost hunting with me, that's what matters." Max's expression was incredibly fond and it made her feel more melty than the chocolate. "The internet might be a long shot, but I bet I know someone who can help us."

"Yeah? If you say it's another subscriber, I will hit you," Shay warned them.

Max had the audacity to laugh in the face of her threat. "No, no, of course not. Remember the place I got that salt from? It's a shop here in town."

"Was that the place with the flute music?" Shay asked. "And all the rocks."

She vaguely remembered cups full of polished stones and a giant tie dye flag on one wall that said something about how standing together was better. She'd honestly been distracted by smelling the hand poured candles and rattling the rocks around, which had gotten them both scolded.

"Yeah!" Max seemed pleased she remembered, at least. "The Good Cauldron. The owner has been running that place for longer than we've been alive. She knows just about all there is to know."

"Dang, and we can't even keep a decent pizza place for two years," Shay said. "All right, yeah, she sounds legit. That's a good idea. Okay, so, Good Cauldron in the morning and possible death in the evening. Yay. Sounds like a fun day."

"Oh, I forgot about that." Max sighed. "Right. Yeah. That's a thing we're doing."

"Don't worry, I'll see the spookums before they come for your face," Shay said. "I mean, no guarantees after that, but I'll give you a heads up."

Max nodded. "And I'll keep you safe."

They sounded very certain of it.

She had to smile. "I know."

Chapter 7:

Spellbound

Shay woke up with sunlight across her face to the sound of Max puttering around the kitchenette.

They'd stayed up late, just talking. She'd veered away from the topic of ghosts and Max obliged, letting her rant about how living with Duncan was the worst. They complained about their dad stomping out the door early in the morning to go to work.

Things weren't really that bad for Shay. Under torture she might even admit that she enjoyed living with her brother. He was annoying, but he let her have control of the tv remote, more often than not. And she hadn't heard a word about her paying rent, though she was sure that would change once she finally found a job.

Max, for their part, had their own little space, even if it was a basement, and they really loved their job.

Venting about the imperfections of an objectively good life was grounding in its normalcy.

Shay fumbled for her phone and found it right where she'd left it – balanced precariously on the arm of the couch. It was nearing noon. She only had one text, from Duncan, reminding her of times, locations, and pizza, along with "you promised!"

and a string of emojis. She groaned and dropped her phone on the floor.

"Good morning!" Max said in sing-song. They appeared above her holding a cup that smelled of spices and warm things. That got her to sit up all the way. They handed off the chai and sat down next to her.

Max, as always, looked incredibly put together. Their hair was already clipped back, their perfect skin was freshly scrubbed, and they were wearing a nice sweater.

"It's too early for you to look this fancy." She huddled around her chai like some sort of gremlin. She probably looked like a wreck, she could practically feel the dark circles around her eyes. The desiccated corpse of her braid hung over her shoulder. Most of her hair had come loose during the night.

"Well, figured I should attempt to make some sort of impression." Max shrugged. The sweater looked really soft. She was tempted to pet it. "How'd you sleep?"

"Eh. Fine." She yawned. There had been nightmares, she remembered snatches of them, but it was hard to hold on to the panicked feeling of a dream when there was hot chai and light spilling through plants crowded on the windowsill.

"And your wrist?"

She held it out. The bruising had faded, not to yellow and brown, but to a faint blue. It didn't hurt when Max touched it. "Pretty much normal, I guess. No arm warmers for me."

"Good." They nodded. "That's very good. I'm guessing you heard from Duncan?"

"Ugh. Yeah." She'd forgotten about that for a moment. She took a sip of her chai to steel herself. It was delicious, as always. "We're on camera duty, sounds like, so it'll probably be boring. Though I guess I can't exactly be like 'hey watch out there's a ghost behind you'. When we go to your witchy store we should get more bath salt, just in case."

Max shrugged. "I guess."

"That wasn't a sarcastic suggestion, that was entirely sincere, you're just used to me being a contrary little gremlin about everything."

Max smiled, pressing their shoulder against hers. "You are not. Sorry. They do have things that are actually for ghosts, you know."

"Um, but what's been tried and tested in the field? Bath salt. Don't mess with a good thing, Max."

"If you keep calling it bath salt you are going to get put on some sort of drug watch list." Max was smiling when they said it.

"I live with Duncan, I'm already there," she said. "Okay, that's not true, he's not that bad. All right, your lavender-infused anti-ghost salt. Is that better?"

"Bit of a mouthful, but I'll take it. You do make a good point, though," they said. "Tried and true lavender-infused anti-ghost salt it is."

"Cool." Shay nodded. "So chai, then magic shop. And then I'll need coffee because I lied about sleeping fine. Finally, pizza."

"Pizza?" Max snagged her braid and began brushing her hair. She didn't mind, really, they probably were better at braiding than she was. They had roughly thirty cousins and Shay was pretty sure braiding parties were mandatory.

"That's what we're getting paid in, remember?" Shay shrugged. "Pizza and nightmares. And the possibility of actual bodily harm, so, it should be a fun evening."

"You do have a knack for making things sound so charming."

"I do, don't I?" Shay finished her chai as Max tied off her braid. "Well. Let's ride."

"Let's."

They were nearly waylaid by Nana, who wanted to tell them all about some drama in her book club. Or it was drama happening in her show. Shay actually wasn't sure, the details got a little muddled for her. They extracted themselves without too much trouble, but a promise to have Shay over for dinner soon.

It was a beautiful Saturday. Late October sunshine lanced down between thick, wooly clouds from a brilliantly blue sky. The trees were all still red and orange, the leaves they had lost clattering down the sidewalks before a cold breeze.

It was hard to believe she would soon be stuck in an old theater, worried about ghosts.

She tried not to think about it, blasting a pop song that Max claimed to hate, but they knew all of the words. The Good Cauldron was in one of the strip malls that bordered downtown. Most stores were in strip malls that surrounded the dead heart of Teton Falls, including two dojos of questionable legitimacy and several sushi restaurants that sprang into being and faded away before Shay got the chance to die eating at one.

This particular specimen featured signs for a Korean BBQ place that was "coming soon" and had been for several years, an old video rental that had never been leased out again, a Used Games that promised it was under New Management, and the store they were actually there for.

Or, at least, where it used to be.

"Aw, man." Max pulled the car into a spot near the front of the door.

It was covered by a sign for a Halloween Super Store.

"Wow, they really moved in fast." Shay peered through the storefront. The shelves were packed with Halloween decorations and there were rows and rows of costumes in plastic bags, just visible through the glass. A witch statue stood outside, green and gnarled. She used a long stick to stir a steaming cauldron and cackled at intervals. "Don't think that's the kind of witch we're looking for."

"Not even close," Max pulled out their phone. "Guess it closed a few weeks ago. That sucks. Now what do we do?"

"Etsy? No, we don't have time for shipping. Well. I guess we can just get salt from anywhere. What about lavender? They have it in tea, would that work?"

"That can be our backup plan." Max tapped their phone. "Here we go. New metaphysical bookstore, Spellbound. Opened up a few weeks ago. How did I miss that? I am so out of the loop."

"For shame, Max. For shame." Shay snagged their phone and started the directions. "Not too far from here, at least. I'm loving the name."

"You would."

"Carries all sorts of witchy stuff, looks like they have rocks, that's the important thing." Shay scrolled through a few pictures of rocks. "Oh, and they help with haunted houses. I think we found a winner."

"How do they help?" Max asked.

Shay shrugged. "I dunno. It's what it says in their description. They have lots of good reviews, so that's nice. Well? Let's go."

Max nodded. "Lead on, young one."

"I'm three months older than you."

They grinned. "You're like a baby in the supernatural world."

"I will ghost eyes you." She pointed from her temples. "Pew pew."

"Terrifying." Max pulled the car out of the parking spot.

Spellbound was in one of the neighborhoods where large, stately houses had been converted into shop fronts instead of sliced up into tiny, sloping apartments. Shay supposed that was more cost effective, but a street of cutesy shops somehow felt worse. At least the strip mall wasn't lying about what it was.

The street was lined with signs that promised cafés and shops in houses that were too large for single people with their pets. The lawns were strewn with Halloween decorations and lights winked from behind jewel toned stained glass windows.

"My aunt and uncle are thinking of buying one of these places and setting up a bakery," Max said. "To sell Leela's cookies."

"What, her Instagram video empire isn't enough for them?" Shay asked. One of Max's many cousins made beautifully decorated cookies. Mostly for social media. Sometimes for weddings or birthday parties on special order. She'd made Shay a cupcake with cute frosting succulents on top when she came back from school.

"Of course not," Max said. "They keep talking about how it would be a great opportunity for me, too, but I like my job? And I cannot be trusted around that many cookies all day."

"Oh, same. I'm glad my family lives far, far away from me," Shay said. Her parents were both professors, so she doubted they'd have any forced employment for her. Maybe grading.

"I don't know if Portland classifies as two fars," Max said. "And what about Duncan?"

"He doesn't count, all he does is make me volunteer at the library sometimes," Shay said.

"Is it volunteering if he makes you do it?" Max asked.

"Fair point," Shay said. "Counter point, he doesn't make me pay rent. And doesn't bother me about getting a job. When my parents start the whole 'take control of your life' thing I can just hang up."

"I wish I could hang up on my parents in real life," Max said. "Best I can do is slam my door."

"Which you won't, you're too nice," Shay said. The phone let her know the destination was on the right. "Woah. Okay. I'm sorry about the cauldron store, but this place looks amazing."

Max pulled up in front of the shop. A sign let them know there was more parking in the back, but Saturday afternoon was apparently the right time to be there. Only a few cars were parked on the street. There was an actual tailor across the street.

Spellbound had been a large, dull red Victorian-style house before its illustrious career as a new age shop began. It had a tower on one side and a porch that wrapped around the front, leaving the door in shadow. Whoever owned the shop was very ready for Halloween. There were bats hanging on the porch, pumpkins on the railing, and skeletons on the roof crawling towards one of the upper windows. Lights had been strung in the windows inside and it glowed invitingly, like the ghoulish cousin of Santa's Workshop.

"I guess it's okay," Max conceded after drinking it all in.

"It's okay," Shay repeated.

Max nodded. "Yeah, I guess."

"Max."

"The Good Cauldron was open for a really long time and everyone there was always nice. They really knew their stuff. This is…I dunno. It's hoity toity."

Shay laughed and they hit her shoulder, gently.

"I'm sorry, but… hoity toity." She pretended to wipe a tear away from her eye. "It's a witch shop—"

"Metaphysical bookstore."

"Whatever, it's going to be a little silly no matter what. C'mon, let's go in before you pass judgment. Judgy McJudgerson. At least it's not in a strip mall," Shay reasoned.

"It had good energy!" Max protested.

"Strip mall energy." Shay opened the door and got out of the car before Max could smack her again, even if she did deserve it. Wind tossed the trees and made the sign hanging over the doorway creak and sway. It reminded her too much of the sale sign at the Johnson House. She shivered and hurried up the walk.

"Hey, wait up!"

"You could hurry up!" She yelled over her shoulder, receiving a glare from a woman coming out of the café next door with her latte and incredibly tiny dog. Or it might have been a rat on a leash. It was hard to tell.

The sign on the door said the shop was open. Shay pushed her way in. A bell above her jangled brightly.

No one else was in the shop.

The interior was dark wood and cream walls. Witch's globes and crystal baubles hung in the windows, catching the light and throwing rainbows on the walls. Most of the store was dedicated to shelves of books, but the back wall had rows of herbs and incense and a display table was heaped with tarot cards, rune stones, candles, and gems left glittering and raw. A shelf on the wall was dedicated to polished rocks. The counter to the right of the door was empty, but soft, ambient chimes were pumped through an invisible speaker system. A candle on the shelf filled the interior with the smell of warm spices.

"Okay, fine." Max had hurried to catch up and walked in practically right behind her. "This place is nice. I'll admit it. Are you happy now?"

"Yes. Extremely." Shay grinned at them and they rolled their eyes.

"Of course, we have no idea how helpful the owner of this place will be," Max said. "I tried messaging the old Good Cauldron page, but I don't know if I'll hear back. Does anyone even work here?"

"I dunno," Shay said. "They have lots of books. Maybe we can just read about the ghosts and call it a day."

"That is a lot of books," Max agreed.

"But salt first," Shay said. "They have to have something similar, right?"

"A lady in Pocatello makes all of the bath salt stuff, looks like they keep the same stuff in stock here." Max led her to the back wall, full of hanging bags with cardboard tags.

Max found it and she struggled not to laugh. The contents were exactly as Max described – salt crystals and lavender. They'd failed to mention exactly what kind of salt it was.

"A love bath, Max? You looking for love in all the wrong places?" She waggled her eyebrows at them. "Is that what all the ghost hunting was for? Did you want to smooch a spirit?"

"No. Shut up." Max's face was darker than usual. They snatched the love bath turned anti-ghost salt and shoved it into a basket they'd grabbed from the front. "Don't be dumb. It just opens you to the suggestion of love. Or something. Whatever. I got it like a year ago and I never used it."

"Aw, why not?" Shay was genuinely curious. They never really talked about dating or crushes, it was the one conversation that Max usually skirted around. Shay so rarely had crushes that it barely ever came up, anyway. "Decided you didn't want to get mushy with someone?"

"Please stop." Max looked just about ready to die. "I just…I didn't use them, okay? It's not a big deal. I don't take baths all that often and. And it doesn't matter."

Shay usually knew when to drop something. "How does the whole salt and herbs thing work, anyway? Just because some lady said it would kick ghost butt? I bet the books know."

"Ghost bad. Salt and herbs good. Boom." Max waved one hand to illustrate the "boom" part of the explanation.

"Max, I'm not five," Shay said.

"Sorry, I talk to a lot of five-year-olds, it's my main go to. Besides, when it comes to this stuff you're basically a baby." Max grinned, but they nodded. "You're right, so, basically humans have been using stuff like salt and lavender for a really long time so…I dunno, I guess they knew what they were doing."

"Or the ceremonies of using lavender and salt for cleansing are so imbedded in the psyche that they have to work." A third voice joined their conversation.

The noises Shay and Max both made were really embarrassing.

There was a woman standing in front of the door marked "employees only". She looked like someone who should run a magic shop – tall, willowy, pale, her long hair dark around the roots. The rest of it was very purple. Big glasses magnified her dark eyes. A string of beads hung down from the frames to loop around her neck. She was probably in her early thirties.

"You just scared the crap out of me," Shay told her.

"Sorry about that." She didn't sound very apologetic. "I'm Jocelyn, this is my shop. We're a little short staffed at the moment. Is there anything in specific you're looking for?"

"Uh, well." Shay exchanged glances with Max.

"We do have some questions," Max said. "About ah. Ghosts. Specifically."

"I can do my best to answer any questions you have," Jocelyn said in a very customer service voice, quite a bit higher pitched than her natural, deeper tone. "Though if you're dealing with ghosts, we do have things for warding your home. We do not carry ouija boards here."

"Oh, not our home. Or their home. Or my home. Either home," Shay said. "No homes. And no boards. We're going ghost hunting at the old theater with a group tonight."

"Ah. You're trying to attract ghosts." She nodded. "Dangerous, but I suppose there is a certain appeal. There are a few candles that might help if you want to conduct a séance, or a few books on meditative techniques if you want to open yourself up to the suggestion. Though I assume you're going in with cameras. Why are you here, exactly?"

"Well, it's not really about that," Max said.

"It's about this." Shay held up her hand. She'd folded back her hoodie sleeve so the blue mark was clearly visible. A line appeared between Jocelyn's eyebrows and Shay hurried to explain before they got tossed out. "So, last night, in a totally legal not breaking and entering sort of deal we were ghost hunting…somewhere else. And I saw a ghost. And it grabbed me. It left a mark. Nothing like that's ever happened, so."

"A ghost grabbed you and you're actually going to haunted places?" Jocelyn sounded almost angry, like Shay's mom when she was giving a lecture. She stepped forward and examined Shay's wrist. "This is…this isn't a bruise."

Shay shook her head. "I thought it was, at first, but it doesn't hurt."

"What kind of ghost…" Jocelyn stared at her arm. "May I?"

"Oh, yeah." Shay nodded.

Jocelyn took her wrist delicately, turning it back and forth. "I have never seen anything like this. But I've heard about it. It's called ghost touch."

"What now?" Shay asked.

"Ghost touch." Jocelyn looked up at her. "I think we have a lot to talk about."

"Yeah." Shay nodded. Something cold and hard settled in the pit of her stomach. "I think we do."

Chapter 8: Ghost Touch

"Okay, tea," Jocelyn said, which was not what Shay had been expecting. "We need tea. And a place to chat that is not my front counter. Flip that sign over for me, will you? Hand me the basket, I'll put it back here."

"Right." Shay turned the sign while Max set the basket almost timidly on the counter.

Jocelyn nodded. "Follow me."

Shay exchanged a look with Max, who shrugged. They walked through the door Jocelyn had come from.

It opened into a bright, clean kitchen. There was a large breakfast nook with a wall of windows that must have been part of the tower she'd seen from outside. Most of it was taken up by a large table, covered in a blue and white gingham tablecloth and surrounded by chairs that looked like they'd sprouted inside the house. There were a few crystals in the windows and plants on the windowsill. A built-in side table was full of jars that didn't look like they contained regular spices.

"Have a seat." Jocelyn indicated the table, grabbing an electric kettle and filling it with water. "I'm sorry, I didn't catch your names."

"I'm Shay, this is Max," she introduced both of them, sitting down at the table a little gingerly. She was certain that she was much, much younger than the piece of furniture.

"You can call me Jo." She pulled out a teapot with a blue design on it, then matching cups, a sugar bowl, and a little milk jug. "Are you both okay with Earl Grey?"

"That sounds fine?" Shay wasn't much of a tea drinker, besides chai. "Are you going to tell me what the whole ghost touch stuff is about?"

"When we have tea," Jo said, a note of finality in her voice. She set out sugar, milk, and a plate of cookies. Shay wanted to make a joke about expecting the queen, but she knew this sort of bustling. Max did the same thing when they were nervous. She let Jo go through her entire tea making and cookie laying ritual without a single smart comment.

Jo finally sat down a few minutes later, pouring each of them a cup of dark tea before filling her own cup. She added a teaspoon of sugar. "Okay. How long ago did the ghost touch you?"

"About sixteen hours ago?" Shay had to check her phone for the time. She fixed her tea with quite a bit more sugar and enough milk the liquid turned from teak to more of a beige. Her spoon chimed against the sides.

"And before that?"

"Didn't really believe in ghosts," she admitted. "I just tagged along with Max to haunted places. They have a show."

"It's nothing big." Max looked embarrassed about it.

"It's called Ghost Town, they have like ten thousand subscribers," Shay said.

"That's really not a lot, Shay," Max said. "It's just for fun."

"I'm familiar with it," Jo said. Max looked like they were contemplating the logistics of trying to drown in a cup of tea. "And clearly you had no idea about your abilities. Tell me everything."

Shay thought this was a lot less of getting an explanation and more of an interrogation, but she told Jo about the ghost and the mirror.

"Well." Jo's hands were shaking and she was on her third cup of tea. She'd brewed a second pot, this time herbal, saying she definitely didn't need more caffeine. "Okay. So. Basically, there are four larger categories of being able to interact with a ghost, and everyone has at least a little bit of one. Touch, hearing, sight, and empathy. Most people have empathy, they can feel the ghost, sometimes even what it's feeling. Hearing is very common. Sight is usually just fleeting glances. I've met very few people who can see ghosts the way you can. Usually they had their abilities enhanced with a charm or a spell…but I've never heard of anyone being able to touch a ghost like that."

"Great. I'm special," Shay said, rubbing her wrist. For a moment it felt like the spectral fingers were still on her skin, despite the warmth of the room and the brightness of the afternoon sunlight glowing through the windows.

She hated that it made sense. The ghost had passed right through Max, giving them nothing but a chill.

She looked down at her cup. Her current cup was golden brown. Less milk. "So what does that make me?"

"And if you've never heard about anyone with touch like that, how did you know what the mark was?" Max asked.

"I don't know, my grandma called them abilities. I haven't seen it, personally, but she said if someone ever came to me with a mark like that, then they have the touch, and I needed to help them." Jo put the cup down on its saucer with a rattle.

"…Your grandma knew I was going to come here?" Shay asked.

Jo smiled thinly. "I come from a family of very talented diviners."

"Wait, like, fortune tellers?" Max asked.

"Exactly like," Jo said. "I come from a long line of witches. And yes, I see you don't believe me, but we're very real. I mostly work with tarot, scrying, some palmistry…"

Shay's head was spinning. She wished she could move her teacup and rest her forehead against the table. "I don't believe in that."

"Which part?" Jo asked.

"The whole…seeing the future thing." Shay waved one hand.

"Oh, no, not the future," Jo said. "Not the way I'm sure you're imagining. Possibilities, yes. But the future isn't something you can just see."

"That makes sense," Max said. At least it made sense to one of them.

"But your grandma knew about me," Shay insisted. "Can I talk to her?"

Jo winced. "Unfortunately, she passed a few years ago."

"Oh. I'm sorry." Shay didn't know how to feel. On one hand, she'd just made a horrible social blunder. On the other, a dead woman had told her granddaughter to watch out for her.

"It's fine." Jo managed a smile, but it looked nervous. "I wish we could call her, too. I'm sure she would know what to do. But, I did promise her, and so I'll promise you. I'm here to help."

"Thank you." Shay didn't know what else to say. What else could she possibly say? "So…you're going to…give me a tarot reading? Palmistry?"

"Palm reading," Jo clarified.

"You can do that?" Shay asked.

"Sure." Jo shrugged.

"That didn't sound very sure."

Jo held out her hand. "May I?"

Shay figured she had nothing to lose. She let Jo take her hand. Very gentle fingers traced over the lines.

"I'm going to be honest with you, I don't do palm reading in the tradition sense," Jo admitted. "But when I'm close to someone like this, it's very easy to get a feel for a person's energies."

"Okay." Shay had no idea what that really meant, but she was beyond scoffing or questioning at that point.

"You have chaos inside of you."

Max didn't actually laugh, but Shay was sure it was a very near thing. Their cough definitely didn't sound natural at all.

"What I mean is, something has changed," Jo explained. "Your life has become very turbulent as of late."

"Well...yeah." Shay thought that was obvious.

"Not just this, though you said you didn't believe in ghosts until last night," Jo said. "A change in world views could lead to some of this, but it's more than that. You've had a lot of changes recently. Did you move?"

"I did," Shay was a little impressed. "Back from college."

"You left for a reason."

Shay frowned a bit. "I hadn't picked a major, so I was thinking of taking a break anyway, but over the summer I kept getting these headaches...so I decided to just stay home."

"I see." Jo nodded. "These headaches. Do you have one now?"

"No." She shook her head.

"And there was never a medical reason for them?"

"How did you know that?" Max asked.

Jo stared, not at her hand, but at Shay's face. She shifted a bit, feeling uncomfortable. "Well. No. Just gave me some meds. Said it was probably stress. What does this have to do with ghosts?"

"Stress might have aggravated it, yes," Jo said. "Trust me, we're getting there. This house where you saw this ghost, what was different about it?"

"The mirror, I guess," Shay said. "Didn't really fit their theme."

"That mirror is bothering me." Jo frowned. "I think it must have something to do with why you can suddenly see ghosts, and why you have such conflicting energy. It's almost like…well, honestly I've never seen anything like this before."

"Awesome." Shay wanted to take her hand back.

"I think you've always had this ability," Jo said. "But something locked it away. That mirror caused a schism in your own energy, which made it seem like a latent power suddenly appeared. What I don't understand is how it was locked away, but I think it's all tied together. I'll have to do some research…the mirror is familiar. There was one in a house just a few miles from here. Arlo took care of it, but it was pretty bad. Ghosts shouldn't be that strong, ever, but lately…"

"Who's Arlo?" Max asked.

"My coworker." Jo's expression was downright grim. She finally let go of Shay's hand. "Look, you can talk about what I do here. It's advertised on the website and everything. But this? I don't want any of this on your little ghost show, okay?"

"Not a problem," Max said, quickly.

"Good." Jo nodded, then sighed. "Sorry. It's been difficult. Arlo does a lot of the…heavy lifting around here. He created the wards and he's the one behind our house cleansing and protection services. Normally, I think he could help you."

"Sensing a but," Shay said.

"Who's the fortune teller now?" Jo smiled, but there was no humor in it. "He's been missing for two days."

"Oh." Shay felt like she'd swallowed a stone.

"He went to clear out a house for a client and… he never came back." Jo stared at her tea cup. "He's not answering his phone. I keep getting calls from people, ghosts are everywhere. But I'm a diviner. I mostly do tarot card readings. Sometimes I find things. I don't deal with ghosts. I'm not that kind of witch."

"What about his family? Does witch stuff run in families?" Shay asked.

Jo shook her head. "Not always. Being a witch isn't about who your family is, except that they can pass down their knowledge and experience to you. Anyone can become a witch, if they want to. Some people are more predisposed towards certain disciplines, and I suppose that can be hereditary. Is anyone in your family particularly sensitive?"

"No?" Shay asked. She thought about it for a moment. Duncan, absolutely not. Her parents, definitely not. There was one person, but she didn't want to think about that. "Well, maybe."

Max gave her a significant look. She knew exactly what they were thinking and shook her head.

Her biological father had left when she was two and never looked back. No calls, no emails, not a single birthday card. Her mom banished all mentions of him and remarried when Shay was five to Conor O'Brannon, who was a pretty okay dad. Especially when he lived several hundred miles away.

"No one I'm in contact with." She wasn't in the mood to be airing out closets just to find the skeletons.

"Then I have no idea," Jo's said. "As for your original question, Arlo's moms are witches, but they live in Ireland. I don't think they're going to be able to help us."

"Seems to be the theme of the day," Shay said.

"You've helped us a lot already," Max said. "We were completely in the dark."

"I doubt I gave you much of a light, but I will do what I can," Jo said. "Two, you are not going to that theater."

"Why not?" Shay asked. She didn't even want to go. "My brother needs us there, I can't just back out now. It's in like three hours."

"Okay, maybe I wasn't clear enough. That's my fault." Jo straightened up a bit. "Let's lay it all out, shall we? The world is going crazy, there are a bunch of powerful ghosts out there, and the only person I know who can deal with them is missing. You are my best hope for finding him, but you want to walk into a potential lion's den. You have ghost touch powerful enough it leaves a mark on your skin. That means ghosts will want to touch you, more than anything. They want to feel something again, and you're it. Congratulations, you're a ghost magnet. One that can be killed by ghosts, very easily."

"That's stupid," Shay said, for lack of anything better to say. "If they can…throttle me or whatever then I should be able to punch them back."

"Yes, well, life is rarely fair." Jo shoved her glasses up to rub her temples. "The important thing here is you can't go to that theater. It's a really bad idea. Spectacularly bad. I don't even think it's a good idea for you to stay anywhere that isn't heavily warded until you get a grasp for what your abilities are and how you got them in the first place."

"Apparently I can grasp ghosts, so we have that down," Shay said. Max sighed and she nudged their foot with hers.

"And we were fine at my place last night," Max said. "Just the ghost in the attic and the one on the road, but I'll just go over the hills from now on. It's safer, anyway."

"Actually…" Shay hadn't mentioned the other ghost. She had caught a glimpse, if she had sat up or hadn't pulled the blanket over her head, she didn't know what would happen. She didn't think anyone related to Max would try to hurt her, but she hadn't ever met the skeleton ghost, either.

"Actually?" Max looked at her.

"Fine. Okay. We're doing this, I guess. I saw a ghost in your apartment. I don't…I don't know. You came in and it went away."

"Oh." Max looked surprised. "You didn't tell me."

"Well, because it was at your desk, you know, and…and I think it was probably…look. I was fine, I just hid under a blanket," Shay admitted. "And once you were back it was gone, so it's probably fine."

Max didn't say anything, but their expression went oddly blank.

"And that doesn't matter, because my brother is going to be at the theater, and if I have abilities and you think it's linked to family, then he probably does, too." Shay turned back to Jo. "He's going with a ghost hunting group, those P.E.I.R.S. guys, so it's probably not even haunted. I mean, I've never heard of anyone dying in the theater."

"Yes, you have." Max latched onto the new conversation.

"There are a few confirmed deaths," Jo said, like it was common knowledge.

"Why do you guys know this?" Shay thought it was a reasonable thing to ask.

"Everyone knows this, Shay," Max said.

"Sure," Shay said. "How many is a few?"

"Three. And a bunch more rumors, but they're probably largely urban legends," Max said.

"Oh, okay, as long as there's only three." Shay felt sick.

"An actress had a light fall on her, it might have been foul play, but no one knows for sure," Max continued without any prompting. "There was a suicide in one of the dressing rooms. Then someone fell off of one of the balconies. It was deemed a freak accident, one of the railings broke, but the theater closed not long after that so who knows."

"Seriously, how do you know this?" Shay asked.

Max gave her a sheepish grin. "Okay, I might have looked it up last night."

"I knew you didn't just know it off the top of your head." Shay sighed, leaning back, but not too far. "Why can't Duncan do something normal for Halloween?"

The enormity of everything was threatening to crush her.

Jo rubbed her temple. "I'm not going to stop you from going, am I?"

"It's not that I really want to," Shay admitted. "It's just…"

"Duncan," Max said. "What if I just went?"

"I wouldn't do that to you," Shay said. "Besides, if there is a ghost, and it…it's going to hurt him, I'll be the one that sees it."

If she could see ghosts on camera, which so far they had no proof she could. She decided to not mention that.

"I wishI could go with you but…I have a group reading I can't cancel tonight. What will you be doing?" Jo asked.

"Just looking at screens," Shay said. "Nothing dangerous. We can make that safe, right?"

She knew it wasn't smart, of course she did.

But Duncan wouldn't believe her. There would be no convincing him to cancel.

"I think so." Jo wrapped her hands around her teacup. "And it wouldn't hurt to have a little more reconnaissance, I suppose. I can give you the tools to stay safe, you use them, and you come right back here. Otherwise…well, I don't know. I actually can't keep you from going. Or keep you here."

"Back here?" Shay asked.

"Arlo and I warded this house ourselves, it's as secure as you'll find in Teton Falls." Jo looked lost in thought for a moment.

A creeping, anxious dread was spreading through Shay, but she knew it would be worse if she canceled, wondering for hours if Duncan was okay while she hid out in a witch's house.

She didn't always get along with him, but he was still her brother.

After a moment, she nodded. "Yeah. That sounds like a plan."

"Great. Go get your things, and I'll get you ready for tonight," Jo said. "Be careful. Ghosts are more likely to be out at night, but…"

Shay nodded.

Their trip back to Max's place was decidedly more subdued.

"I really think I should just go," Max said after a few minutes. "I can use Jo's stuff to keep Duncan safe."

"I wouldn't ever make you do that," Shay said.

"Ghosts can't hurt me, Shay, but they can hurt you. Maybe you should stay at Jo's. I'm not even letting you back in my place. I can't believe you didn't tell me."

They sounded hurt and she felt guilty all over again. "Yeah, I know. I just didn't want to be like 'so I saw your dead grandpa, want to watch a movie?' It sounded, well I dunno. Bad. And a terrible conversational segway. Look, we're going to be fine. These P.E.I.R.S. guys are professionals, right?"

"I mean, they're a ghost hunting group that operates out of Doveton," Max said. "So… about as professional as they can be, I guess. On second thought, let's not go, actually. I don't want to run around with a bunch of 'professionals' and you won't get hurt. Duncan can handle it."

"Duncan could also get hurt," Shay said. "Or worse. If there's even a chance he has a ghost thing, too, I think I have to be there. Besides, I thought you'd be more excited to meet a bunch of real ghost hunters."

"Any excitement I would have had is sort of overshadowed by the whole my best friend could get hurt or killed thing. Besides, I have met them," Max said. "Well, kinda. The founder emailed me once? He wanted to talk to me about possibly joining the team. I said no, so…it's going to be really, really awkward and this was a mistake."

"What!" Shay slapped the dashboard. "Max! You didn't say anything? And why would you say no? You would have been so good!"

"I dunno," Max shifted uncomfortably. "Look… yeah. Ghost hunting is fun, and it'd be cool to have all of their equipment and a team and stuff, but I like going with you."

Shay was floored. For a moment she couldn't say anything, and the next words out of her mouth made her want to sink into her seat and disappear forever. "But I'm a butt."

"You're not a butt, you're my best friend," Max said. "And even though you didn't believe you still went with me, and that mattered. It was our thing."

"We could have found other things," Shay said. She had no idea it meant that much to Max. The entire time she'd thought she was just tagging along and being at the very least low-grade annoying.

"I mean, yeah, but, well, I don't know." Max shrugged. They'd stopped at a red light. "I didn't want things to change, I guess. I didn't want to mess things up, you know? It wasn't perfect but it was fun. With you."

"Aw Max." She patted their arm. They'd joked about it a little bit the night before, but she supposed the ghost hunting with Max era of her life really was over. It was strange, it felt like it had just begun and it was ending at the same moment. Things always seemed to be that way – the moment she thought she had it figured out, everything was already finished and she was left picking up the pieces. "That's really sweet, but you know I'm a disaster. If I can't mess it up, then someone like you definitely can't. No matter what we're doing or what happens, that's never going to change, even if we can't go anymore."

Max smiled. "Thanks, Shay."

"And you're a big sap but I love you anyway," Shay said, quickly. "And if you want to join the ghost hunting gang, then you should! I promise I won't be offended, even though I had fun, too. But…"

Max risked the light turning green and gave her a quick side hug. "We'll find other things, I promise. You're my favorite person in the world."

"Aww you." She felt lighter for the first time that day. Maybe not everything ended the moment she figured it out. "You're mine, too."

True to their word, Max didn't let her go back into the apartment. They were gone for almost twenty minutes before they left with her bag and one of their own.

"You going somewhere?" Shay asked.

"I'm not letting you stay in the witch house by yourself," Max said. "We just had this talk. Besides, we don't know Jo. I mean, she seems really cool, but yeah. No. That's not happening."

"Our new thing is sleeping in nearly perfect stranger's houses?" Shay asked. "Why Max, that's so daring."

"I live on the edge," Max said, seriously. They both laughed a moment later and it felt like things were swinging back to normal. "Do you think Jo is overreacting? Do you think something is happening?"

Or not quite as normal as she'd hoped. "Why would I know? Maybe that Arlo guy just bounced. It happens. I don't know him so I can't really say. Maybe…he ghosted her."

"Ugh," Max said. "Still, two mirrors, two ghosts? Seems like a little too much to be coincidence, don't you think?"

Shay shrugged. "Coincidence happens all the time. But I'll admit, this might be a little too much."

"Me, too."

Once they were back at Jo's she put them to work in the kitchen, showing them how to measure out sachets and tie them properly.

"These will help. I'm sending you with some crystals, too," she said. "And yes, the salt, since you seem to think it was so helpful."

"It was!" Shay reminded her.

"Right, right." Jo waved one hand. "I'm going to make sandwiches."

She'd already made them more tea and put out crackers. Shay had a feeling that she combatted her anxiety by feeding people, which was not the worst quality for a potential future roommate to have. Even if it was only for a few days.

Hopefully.

Shay finished the last sachet and tossed it into the basket, missing and hitting Max. Outside the sun was setting, throwing long, dark shadows through the streets. It was time to head to the theater.

Jo was preparing for her group reading when they left the kitchen. A table had been set up in the middle of the open space, surrounded by chairs that clearly hadn't been salvaged from anywhere that wasn't an antique store. "Heading out?"

"Yup, have all of the sachets." Shay pointed to the basket Max was holding. "Are you going to be okay?"

"This is what I'm good at," Jo said. "I'll be fine. You two, stay safe, call me if anything happens. Literally anything. I can be there right after the reading."

"Okay. Thanks, Jo," Shay said. "We'll see you in a few hours."

CHAPTER 9:
P.E.I.R.S.

few of the decorative streetlamps flickered to life, buzzing like late season insects. Most of them stayed dark. The old Explorer's tires bounced over potholes and cracks that the city couldn't bother to repair. Downtown looked bad during the day. At night, it was oppressive.

The theater was the exception, standing impressive even in the dark. Thick, white columns flanked the doors, Community Theater embossed in faded gold letters across an entrance built to look like a Greek temple.

The side wasn't quite as impressive. Just a weedy parking lot that had seen better days and the brick bulk of the building. They pulled into a parking spot next to a large, black van that must have belonged to P.E.I.R.S. Duncan's little compact was on the other side.

"I'm kind of disappointed they don't have a logo on the side." Shay looked at the van. It was completely nondescript. It looked more like a surveillance van for some government agency than a ghost hunting mobile.

"I'm pretty sure the main guy uses that to go to his job," Max said.

"Well, he should own the whole ghost hunting thing a little more," she said. "Really lean into it."

She went to open the door but Max's hand on her shoulder stopped her.

"Hey um. It's gonna be okay," they said. "But I had Jo grab this for you, just in case."

They handed her a sachet.

"Is this one special?" she asked. Jo had stuffed a bag full of protective sachets made of unbleached linen. This one was small, dark green, and velvety.

"It's a little more um. Oomphy. Has stones Jo said were good for keeping away ghosts," Max explained. "You can even wear it like a necklace, see?"

They pulled out the string until it was long.

"Thanks." She looped it over her neck, tucking it under her hoodie. "Well. Better get in there, I guess. What's our distribution plan? I'm thinking we shove them in people's pockets when they're not paying attention.

"Yeah, sure." Max looked like they'd rather do literally anything else, but they got out of the car with her, grabbing the backpack full of satchets. "Wait, no! We're not doing that. How about if things get bad, we hand them out? You and Duncan will probably need them more than anyone else."

"Fine, I suppose," Shay said. "If you want to be boring."

"I do. I really, really do."

They walked over to the side entrance. The van's back doors were open to it. Light spilled over the cracked concrete.

"Hey!" A skinny, pale man who looked too old to have a man bun and thick, horn-rimmed glasses was setting up a camera just inside the door. He was wearing a black t-shirt with "P.E.I.R.S." emblazoned in white across the chest. It even had a little ghost. "Max, good to see you again! And you must be Shay."

"That's me." She nodded.

"I'm Vic, great to meet you." He held out a hand. Max shook it, Shay pretended it hadn't been for her. "And that Max decided to come by tonight. We like your moxie, kid."

He was older than she thought, but Shay was delighted by his use of the word "moxie", anyway. "I am particularly fond of the cut of their jib."

"Oh, absolutely." Vic went back to angling the camera to record down a dark hallway that could have belonged to an office building. "All right, really this is to make sure no one sneaks in here tonight, but you never know."

He wiggled his fingers in a way that was probably supposed to be spooky.

"Where are we all set up?" Max asked.

"A little tour, first! Before we get started!" Vic had way too much energy for a man probably old enough to be her father, practically bounding inside.

"Oh, um, okay," Max said, looking at her. "He's uh. Excited."

"I think it's awesome," she said. "I wanna be like that when I'm an old lady."

"You're going to break both of your hips falling off a hoverboard or something when you're old," Max said. "Guaranteed."

"And then I can be a bionic old woman." Shay nodded. "Maybe they'll install some lasers or something cool."

"I will tell them to not do that."

"Spoilsport." She elbowed them. "At least you've got moxie, kid."

"Shut up," Max groaned. She cackled and hurried after Vic to avoid getting elbowed herself.

The back of the theater was full of hallways that looked vaguely like the labyrinth that led to the professors' offices when she was at school. White walls and dusty ceiling tiles.

The lobby was a different story. It held onto the faded glamor of the theater's glory days, barely visible in the light of a handful of storm lanterns set up around the room. A plush rug, gray with dust, covered the white marble. Large swaths of dull red marked where equipment had been dragged across it. Faded posters lined the walls, leading the way to an ornate ticket counter under a corroded sign that Shay couldn't read. Cobwebs and dust softened the edges of the empty room.

The air felt colder.

"You had to at least see the lobby. We're set up on stage, c'mon." Vic motioned to them. "Unless you want to see the dressing room? You probably know the one, Max."

"I do, but I think we're good," Max said. "Don't want to contaminate the scene."

"Right you are, right you are," Vic said. "So good to be working with another professional."

Shay grinned and elbowed them gently again. They flushed a dark red.

Vic led them into the theater itself.

The stage had been made easily accessible from the audience, so actors could run down the aisles. Empty seats spread out around them and Shay tried very hard to keep her eyes on the floor, but the occasional glance, even with the poor lighting, made her expect to see someone sitting in the sagging and broken seats, waiting in the dark.

No one was, but she swore it was even chillier. High above them the wind made the building groan and creak.

"Bad weather for ghost hunting," Vic said. "Anything could be a breeze or a spirit, but we gotta say it was a breeze."

There was already a camera on the stage, but they were farther back, behind filthy dark red curtains. More curtains, absolutely festooned with cobwebs hung in thick shrouds from the ceiling. Dust coated the stage.

"And welcome to base!" Vic gestured towards it. "I have other cameras to set up, but I'm sure I'll see you kids before we start!"

And he left them to make their way to it. Shay exchanged a glance with Max, who shrugged.

"Base" was a horseshoe of long folding tables. There were three laptops and a full monitor, all plugged into a little generator that hummed nearby. Another table had a stack of pizza boxes, soda, and a coffee maker.

"Hey, you guys made it!" Duncan stopped talking to a tall black man with thick, tight curls. They were both wearing P.E.I.R.S. shirts and Shay tried to not be jealous. "This is Gideon! Gid, this is Shay and Max."

"Ah, yeah, I know Max," Gideon said. "Vic tried to recruit them last year. Love your stuff."

"Vic did mention Max's moxie." Shay knew she was being a brat, but she was absolutely delighted that several people were complimenting Max's hobby. Even if they didn't plan to keep up with it. They deserved the recognition.

"We do, in fact, quite like it." Gideon laughed. "Duncan, how about you help Meri with the cameras while I show them around base?"

He gestured to a pale woman with an incredible undercut who was adjusting a few things on the table. She rolled her eyes, but nodded.

"You got it." Duncan gave Gideon finger guns. He was clearly besotted. "Listen to him, you two!"

"We will." Shay thought about flipping him off, but settled on waving as sarcastically as she could. She was supposed to be playing wing person, after all.

"He's been a great help, I'm super stoked that we're working with the library," Gideon said. "We've been wanting to investigate it for years, great old building. Anyway, let me show you guys what we're doing. If you have fun, maybe you can come along on a few of our scarier research trips."

"Would we get cool t-shirts?" Shay asked, ignoring Max trying to elbow her discreetly.

"Oh, you guys can have a cool t-shirt for helping us out tonight. We have a ton." Gideon gestured to a box. "Just snag your size. Okay, spiel time. The Paranormal Eastern Idaho Research Society, or P.E.I.R.S., is dedicated to finding and contacting those that have passed beyond. We try to do this with as much sensitivity and respect as we can, using the latest technology. Okay, so, that's out of the way. You guys will be keeping an eye on base here, making sure we check in and making sure the cameras are working. You'll have access through the laptops and the monitor. It's mostly easy, but it can get kind of boring and you have to stay alert, so utilize that coffee pot or the soda as much as you need."

Shay nodded. "Consider them utilized."

"Cool. Like I said, it's pretty easy. Just keep an eye out and you can contact us on the radio there if you need to," Gideon said. "It's already set to the right channel and everything. And that's about it. Any questions?"

"How did you get into ghost hunting? I mean paranormal research?" Shay asked. "Did you see a ghost?"

"Yeah, actually." Gideon looked a little surprised that she'd asked. "When I was a kid. Saw an old lady climbing the stairs of the house my parents moved into. It got pretty bad, actually, we had to call someone in. I've been in the business pretty much ever since. I used to live up in Montana, got really into it there. Moved here for a job and joined P.I.E.R.S. Vic's been really welcoming everyone in the group is really cool. What about you guys?"

"Oh yeah, saw a ghost," Shay said. She decided to not mention it had been a little less than twenty-four hours ago. "It looked like a skeleton, wearing a suit. Came out of an old mirror in an attic."

She also didn't mention it had dragged her across the floor, tucking her hands in her pockets to hide the faint marks on her wrist.

"I mean, I've always been interested. I used to watch a bunch of shows with my Nana. But my first ghost? I was twelve. It was at a birthday party. Shay's, actually," Max said. They'd told her this story before, but she hadn't really had the context of "ghosts are real" at the time. "You fell asleep and I went to get a glass of water. Someone was standing at the sink. It was dark, and they were just a darker shape. I thought it might be Duncan, so I asked what he was doing. He didn't answer. I got scared and turned on the lights, but no one was there."

"Eugh." Gideon shivered. "I'd be calling my mom to pick me up right away. I'm not going to be the first to die in a horror movie. Well...yeah, okay, now I probably am. It's just interesting, y'know? Besides, ghosts can't hurt you. Vic has been doing this for decades and the worst that's happened to him were some scratches."

"Yeah, but he's a white dude," Shay reminded him.

"Too true." Gideon grinned at her. She could see where Duncan was coming from, he was handsome and easy to talk to. She mentally gave him her stamp of sisterly approval. "Oh, Taylor is here! We're going to have a team huddle soon. You guys are part of the team tonight, so don't miss it!"

Taylor walked up to the stage. She a few inches taller than Shay and curvy enough she could tie her over-sized PIERS shirt in a knot at her hip and it looked good. Her long brown hair tumbled over her shoulders. Her skin was milk white, the pink of her lips bordering on garish in comparison.

Gideon bounded over to her and pulled her into a big bear hug that lifted her off of her feet.

She laughed. "Wow! Someone's happy to see me!"

"You've missed the last three investigations, we're all pretty happy to see you." Meri's hug was more reserved and to the side.

"Man, it's been ages," Gideon said. "I can't believe you missed out on the old courthouse."

"I am really sad I missed it," Taylor said. "Work has been insane. But I'm here tonight! I missed you, too. We should get coffee, soon. Like, really soon. Like…right now. Oh! New recruits?"

"This is Duncan O'Brannon." Gideon gave Duncan a kind of goofy smile. Shay hadn't really talked him up or attempted any sort of wing persons duties, but it didn't look like she really needed to. Maybe it was Duncan's dumb hair, carefully sculpted tonight in a way that looked like he spent no time at all on it. "He works at the library. And manning our camera stations is Shay. And Max! Max Patel. I'm sure you've heard of them."

"I have! Hello, Max, lovely to meet you." Taylor shook Max's hand first with a delighted smile.

"Nice to meet you," they repeated. "I've seen some of your pictures, you're amazing with a camera."

"I try! Thank you, that's so nice, especially coming from you" Taylor beamed at them. "And of course it's nice to meet you too, Shay."

Her hand was cold when Shay shook it. Shay barely kept herself from wiping her hand on her jeans when they let go. Taylor gave her a different smile than Max, like the two of them were sharing a secret.

Taylor turned to shake hands with Duncan, but the odd feeling lingered. "And Duncan! The one who made it all possible. We've been wanting to do a hunt here for ages."

"Ah it was nothing." Duncan grinned. "Gideon is really the one to thank, he talked the whole group up at the Pride event to me."

"Yeah, he's pretty all right." Taylor punched Gideon's arm, lightly. "We'll keep him around, for now. Where's Vic? Isn't it about huddle time?"

"He's in the back, setting up the rest of the cameras," Gideon said. "Should be any minute now."

A minute or so later Vic emerged from the back of the theater, bouncing on the balls of his feet, followed by a large red-faced man with a crew cut and glasses that looked vacuum sealed to his head.

"Taylor!" Vic pulled her into a hug. "Wow, we weren't sure you'd show up! This is great! Whole team, plus new friends, and this lovely old theater! What a night!"

The man with Vic was content to wave and wait for introductions, which were much more brief than Taylor's. His name was Sam and they had his normal job for the night.

"Okay, team, assignments!" Vic clapped his hands. "I'm gonna have Gideon and Duncan in the dressing rooms to start. It's super spooky back there, you'll have a blast! Meri, Tay, you're gonna be up in the balcony. Also spooky! Sam and I are gonna be in the front area and going to start with EVP over in the seats, so keep it to a dull roar over here."

"We'll do our best." Shay gave him a thumbs up.

"Yeah, love that attitude! Okay, you know the drill. You need anything, you contact Shay and Max at base. They're gonna be here all night," Vic continued. "If stuff gets intense head back this way, remember, no shame. We're respectful of ghosts, but more importantly we respect each other. Pizza and coffee for all, but if you take the last cup make a new one or we will leave you locked in the dressing room. Any questions?"

Vic looked at them like he expected them to have questions.

"No questions," Meri said when it was clear he was still waiting.

"Cool cool!" Vic pumped one fist in the air. "Then huddle up, guys, gals, and nonbinary pals!"

They did the cheesy thing where they put their hands in the middle of the circle and raised them. Afterwards the teams split off into their assignments. Shay grabbed a plate of pizza and sat down, looking at the monitors. Some of the camera feeds were tinted green while others were infrared, layers of blue and purple with red and orange highlights filling their section of the screen.

Max sat down without pizza, carefully tucking their backpack under the table.

Shay grinned at them. "They like your stuff! That's awesome!"

"It's just my phone and some free editing software." Max shrugged. "It's not exciting. I'm gonna set up the ward stuff."

"I think it's cool. A lot of people think it's cool, but my opinion is most important. You want help?" she set down her plate.

"No, I got it."

They were silent for a few minutes while Max put crystals under tables where they couldn't easily be seen. If it changed anything, Shay couldn't tell.

Max tossed her a sachet and sat down, fiddling with their own.

"Y'know, I meant it, if you want to join them that's totally cool," Shay said. "We can find...safer things to do. Like rock climbing. Or kayaking? I'm not sure why I keep listing outdoor activities. I guess we could start with hiking. Geocaching? Is that a thing still."

"Yes, it is, and that's super cool of you," Max sighed. "I'm just sad! Because this is the last time we're ghost hunting together. Y'know?"

"Awww Max don't be sad, be happy, this'll be fun." Shay smacked their foot with her own. "You're too nice to me. But, speaking of nice, they all seem nice."

"Yeah, they do." Max smiled at her. "And that Taylor seemed to think you were kinda cute."

"Aww what? No." Shay felt strange about that. "Talk about bad taste."

"Don't sell yourself short!" Max laughed.

"Was that a short joke? A pun!" She gasped. They were busy laughing at their own terrible joke, which she supposed was fair. "Max! I can't believe you! You can't use puns against me! That's the worst form of pun-ishment."

"Oh no now I regret everything." Max was still smiling. "Fine, but I think you're a great person and a good friend."

"I think you're a big sap," Shay said.

"Yeah, only for you. Grab our shirts, we should wear them, right?"

"Oh yeah!" She yanked the box out from under the table and began digging through piles of carefully folded black shirts. "Let's see, XL for Extra Love for you… and one for me!"

She grabbed a medium for herself and tossed Max's shirt to them. She unzipped her hoodie and pulled it on over her band shirt. "Now I will be warm."

Max did the same. "Come over here, there's a space heater and we can huddle."

"I do like a good huddle cuddle," she said. She didn't bother to fold the shirts she'd rummaged through, shoving the box back under the table with her foot. They sat together in front of the bank of monitors. "We're all safe now. Snug as bugs. Not in a rug because the rugs in here are disgusting. Okay. What do we do here? You're the expert, I am deferring to you."

Max nodded. "What we're doing is watching for weird movement on all of these. See the little boxes? Those are motion sensor lights. If they light up then something is potentially in the room. I can take these two laptops, you take the monitor and the last one. Watch for weird movement, or on the thermal-"

"Heat vision?" Shay asked.

"Heat vision, sure." Max shrugged. "You watch for cold spots, blobs of blue or purple. Or even for hot spots. Some ghosts can do that. Basically, if anything is moving that isn't an obviously an animal or one of the teams moving through."

"Got it." Shay gave them a thumbs up. "I can do that."

The night went on. They talked about a video game that Max was finally playing that she'd beaten years ago. Teams checked in on occasion, saying they were heading to the orchestra pit or the dressing rooms. Occasionally she saw them moving on the cameras, either like ghosts themselves on night vision or glowing red or yellow like they were made of fire on the infrared.

Duncan and Gideon were the first ones to come through for more coffee.

"Watch out, Gideon, there's a hideous ghost behind you," Shay said.

Duncan laughed sarcastically and rolled his eyes. "Hilarious."

"I dunno, he's not that hideous." Gideon flashed him a smile and Duncan grinned back, goofily. Any wing person skills she may have possessed were clearly not necessary. "The shirts look great!"

"Thanks!" Shay spread her arms. "They're cool shirts."

"Well, thank you. How are the cameras? Anything going on?"

"Nothing yet," Max said. "But it's still pretty early."

"Cool, keep us posted."

Shay was getting more coffee for herself when Max leaned forward, a crease appearing between their eyebrows. "That's weird."

"What's weird?" Shay asked.

Instead of answering, Max grabbed the radio. "Hey, Vic? The camera in the dressing room is picking up something. Are any of you in the area?"

"No." Vic's voice came through in a garble of static. "We're all up in the balcony seating. Can one of you grab a hand cam and check it out? Could be something exciting."

Max and Shay looked at each other.

"Yeah. Yeah, I can go." Max's face was already drained and scared. "I'll be right back. Shay, don't leave."

"You got it, Captain Max." Shay saluted them with her Styrofoam cup. "You sure you won't need backup?"

"I am absolutely sure." Max sounded like they had never been less sure of anything in their life. "You should stay here. I'll be okay."

They grabbed a hand camera, a flashlight, and the spare radio, took a deep breath, and strode out into the dark.

Shay was impressed. She'd have to tell them that when they got back, though she was expecting a lot of screaming to come through the radio at any moment.

Being alone was worse than she expected. She hurried back to the monitors so she could see what Max was talking about in the dressing room. It looked like someone was in there on the infrared, if people showed up much colder than a dressing room that hadn't seen a heater in several years and moved in wild and erratic jerks.

She winced. Hopefully it was just a weird air current or something.

She was distracted from the display when another one of the monitors went out. It took a moment of fumbling with the radio to get it to hiss to life. "Um, Vic? The stage camera went out. What do I do?"

"Ah, damn." Vic sounded pretty upset. "The one on the other side of the curtain?"

"Yup," Shay confirmed.

"Battery must have died, it happens," Vic said. "That's one of the hot spots. Or cold spots. You see the bank of batteries charging next to the computer?"

"Yeah?" She said it before she thought to lie about it.

"Okay, it's only about thirty feet away from you, so you should be fine to go change it," Vic said. "Just the other side of the stage. Do it quick and report when you get back to base."

"Um…copy that?"

Vic laughed a bit. "You'll be fine. Just pop out the old battery bank and shove the new one in. Click clack. Easy peasy."

"Okay. I can do that."

It was stupid, but it was also so close it seemed even worse to wait until Max was back. Especially since they hadn't even reached their destination. Just to be safe, she grabbed a few sachets, shoved them in her pockets, and tucked the bag of anti-ghost salt under her arm.

Feeling as ready as she possibly could be, a storm light in one hand and a battery in the other, she headed to the front of the stage. The whole area was much bigger than she'd thought, the curtains really hid just how large it was. Then again, at one point it had held sets, props and actors.

It was darker than she expected it to be. All of the lights that led to base had been turned off for the investigation. She made it through the curtain. A faint glow came from one of the seats, towards the back. She watched it out of the corner of her eye, but it didn't do anything or take any shape, just hovered in place. Maybe if she didn't acknowledge it then it wouldn't notice her, either.

It still felt like it was watching her, the cold itching feeling creeping up her neck.

The camera was trained on a part of the stage that didn't look any different than the others, but must have been where the light fell. She made her way to it, carefully. Her shoulders felt like they were trying to lock up around her ears. The building moaned, low and loud, all around her.

"Just the wind," she whispered to herself.

After setting the lantern down, the bag of salt next to it, she tried to figure out how the battery came out. Away from the space heater at base it was freezing. Her fingers didn't want to find the latch.

Finally, it slid out and she set it on the stage, just as she heard something moving beyond the curtain.

Footsteps.

She froze for a moment. It took all of her willpower to quietly grab the bag of salt and rise from her crouch until she was standing, absolutely silent.

The footsteps drew closer and something moved the curtain aside. She squeezed her eyes shut and threw the salt out in a wide arc, hoping it would catch whatever was bearing down on her.

Chapter 10: Dead Batteries

"Ow!"

Shay was pretty sure ghosts didn't say ow. She opened one eye.

Duncan was brushing rock salt and lavender off his clothes. "What the hell? What was that for? Is this salt?"

"Did you think we were ghosts?" Gideon seemed to think it was funny. Probably because Duncan had taken the brunt of the attack.

"Of course I thought you were ghosts!" Shay shook the bag at him. Her voice had gained an octave and shook tremulously. "You can't just go… why are you sneaking around back here!"

"Vic said you were taking a while, so we came to check on you," Gideon said.

Duncan brushed off more salt. "And to think I was worried about you. Ugh what are these? Bugs?"

"It's dried lavender," she said.

"Looks like bugs." Duncan shuddered. "Why do you have…you know what? I don't care. I don't want to know. Just change the battery and let's go, okay?"

"Okay. Sorry," she said. She didn't mean it.

"Yeah, we found her. We're heading back to base," Gideon said into the radio. He took the battery from her. "I'll get it in there, it can be a little tricky, no matter what Vic says."

"Thanks." She nodded. She was pretty sure she was going to start crying in a second and she really, really didn't want to do that. "Sorry."

"No worries, we were heading back to base anyway. You're perfectly fine," Gideon said, his voice a little gentler. "Duncan has a headache."

"More like a migraine." Duncan pressed a hand to the back of his neck. "What about you, nerd, your head feel like it's about to split?"

"No, I-" Shay's voice died in her throat.

A woman was floating behind the camera, so close that Shay could have reached out and touched her.

She was the same cold, dull blue that Shay was starting to associate with ghosts. She was beautiful. Her hair spilled in ringlets down her back. Her dress, something Victorian and heavy, didn't quite reach the floor, fading out into mist that spread underneath her. She faced the dark rows of empty seats, expression serene, her hands held out to them like she was about to sing to a nonexistent audience. The lantern flickered and died, but blue light filled the stage with more brilliance than any battery powered light could hope to achieve.

"What is that?" Duncan's voice broke through the silent spell that engulfed them.

The woman rotated towards them. The other side of her head was caved in, the curtains visible through the space where her face should have been.

She surged towards them. Shay flung the remaining salt at her, as hard as she could. It sparked blue and green. The ghost didn't seem to notice, scrabbling at her face.

Shay grabbed her wrists. They felt like dry sticks and the cold burned into her hands. What was left of the woman's face was twisted into something that didn't look like it could have ever been human, the mouth a downturned slash, the eye a pinpoint of light.

She yanked Shay up like she weighed nothing and slammed her onto her back. The air burst from her lungs. The freezing weight of the ghost threatened to crush her.

Then it was gone, reeling away from her like it had been burned. She lay there for a moment. Her palms burned like she'd set them on frozen metal.

"Shay!" Gideon was helping her up. His other hand was holding the video camera, trying to keep it trained on the ghost. "Oh my god, what. What was that?!"

"I'm fine! Duncan—"

Her brother was kneeling too far away from them. His head was in his hands. There was no sign of his flashlight.

The ghost tipped her head back and roared.

The sound filled the building. It shook the rafters and vibrated in Shay's bones. Wind screamed around them. Curtains ripped from their housings, swirling the stage like demented bats. Dust whipped into a frenzy.

Through it all was a large mirror, tucked into the back. Its surface was black. Mist tumbled over the lip.

"Cover the mirror!" She yelled at Gideon, for all the good it did. She doubted he could hear her. She shoved a sachet in his hands.

She had to help Duncan.

Getting to him was a painstaking process. He was only a few feet away, but she had to walk against the wind. A curtain nearly knocked her off of her feet. She tightened her grip on the sachet, holding an arm over her eyes, ducking her head, and walking forward.

The ghost had the same idea.

The wind changed direction so abruptly Shay nearly fell. The ghost rushed past her in an icy blast. Her hair floated around her like a halo. She disappeared, but the wind only got worse.

"No!" Shay couldn't even hear her own voice.

Duncan looked up and the ghost reappeared in front of him. She reached out to touch him.

Shay didn't have time to think.

She had a sachet in one hand, but the salt hadn't done anything. She doubted the herbs would be any more effective.

But they were her only weapon.

She took the last few steps and jabbed her fist into the ghost's back.

It felt like punching a thin sheet of ice. Her hand plunged into intense cold. Bright blue and green flames erupted around her fist. The woman burned apart from the inside, a final scream echoing around the theater, shaking the rafters.

The wind stopped abruptly. Curtains fell in heavy clumps. Dust drifted through the air, the stage a horrible nightmare of a snow globe.

Shay opened her hand and the sad remains of the sachet crumbled out of her fingers.

"Oh my god." Gideon stared at her. "You just punched it out of existence. Oh my god."

Shay knew they had to move, but she felt gutted. Her hands ached. She curled them up to her chest. Her legs shook too much to stand and she kneeled on the stage.

"Shay?" Duncan put his hands on hers. His fingers felt like brands. "Shay, what just happened? My head hurt and then…"

"It was a ghost!" Gideon yelled, which made both of them wince away. "And you just…you punched it!"

"We need to get to base." Duncan stood up, pulling Shay with him. "She's freezing."

"She can hear you," Shay protested. Her voice was shakier than before.

"Good, then she can probably walk on her own." Duncan put an arm around her shoulders, anyway. "When we get back you are explaining everything."

"You fell on the floor," Shay reminded him.

"So did you!" He looked pale, but she couldn't immediately see anything wrong with him. "My head was killing me. I dunno, but it went away when the lady did. C'mon. Where did my flashlight go?"

At some point the lantern had tumbled off the stage. She shouldn't have been able to see Duncan at all.

She looked down at their feet. Mist was eddying around their ankles. The mirror was still dark, the edges glowing an almost virulent green.

White fingers gripped the edge of the frame. She cringed away from it. She couldn't breathe. It was too cold.

"What is that?" Duncan asked.

Ghosts spilled out of the mirror. Shay looked wildly for the skeleton, but if it was there, she couldn't see it. The ghosts were all ages and shapes, dressed in every period of clothing. Some of them had barely any defining features at all. Some a dull blue. Others were so bright it hurt her eyes.

"Here." She slapped the second to last sachet on Duncan's chest. She had one left, so she had to make it count. She was still shaking, but she held her hands out in front of her anyway. She was ready. If the skeleton tried to drag her back she would give it something to worry about.

The ghosts swirled around them. Some separated into their own entities, others stayed an amalgam of limbs, scuttling spider-like towards her. She screamed and swung her sachet. They backed away, but not far enough.

Duncan sagged against her shoulder. He felt impossibly heavy.

"I don't feel good," he murmured. "Shay-"

"C'mon, Donuts, base, remember?" Shay asked.

"I got him." Gideon only sounded slightly less panicked than she did. He grabbed Duncan's shoulder and pulled him upright.

Just in time. One of the ghosts darted forward. Shay swung and it connected. The blue green fire consumed the ghost and it disappeared in a flash. The sachet was dust in her palm. She swung at the next ghost, anyway. Her hand sunk into the its torso like it was made of heavy, wet clay. It staggered back. Her hand pulled free with a horrible, sucking sound.

"Hey!"

Salt sprayed around her. The ghosts around her hissed and screamed, retreating for the mirror.

"Max." She couldn't remember ever being happier to see them, holding a flashlight and half a bag of salt, their expression wild. "I—"

Something knocked into her. She hit the stage, hard enough to knock the air out of her lungs. A pale figure flowed past her. Max shouted and threw more salt, but it wasn't aiming for her. Or for them.

It went straight at Duncan, brilliant and blinding. It hit him and disappeared like smoke.

"What was that?" Gideon's voice had gone squeaky with fear. He was helping Shay up. He was too warm. Or she was too cold. She couldn't breathe.

"Duncan?" Max asked, quietly.

"Hm. Not the worst name I've been called." Duncan was speaking, but the cadence was off, like an accent she couldn't identify was trying to slip through. He straightened Duncan's cardigan, smoothing a hand over the material.

When he looked at her his eyes, normally a dark brown, were a dull blue. "Ah. Siblings. That makes sense."

"Duncan…?" Gideon sounded hesitant to even say his name.

"Who are you?" Shay finally found her voice. And her feet. She stood up and faced him. "Get out of my brother."

"Is that really important?" Duncan smiled, or at least Duncan's body did. It wasn't the goofy, crooked smile of her idiot brother. It was sinister, frigid, and didn't reach his too pale eyes. He looked at his fingers, opening and closing them in a fist like he hadn't had fingers in a long time. "Oh, yes, this is going to do quite nicely."

"What are you talking about?" Shay wanted to scream. She wanted to throw things at Duncan until it was him again, but there was nothing but scattered salt. "Whoever you are, you'd better get out, or I—"

"You'll what?" Duncan looked back up at her. "Oh, little ghost hunter, you're way more out of your depth than you realize."

He walked past her. She lunged for him, but he sidestepped her easily. He looked back once he reached the mirror. "I'd say goodbye but it's more of a see you very soon."

He grinned again and stepped through the mirror.

The ghostly light filling the room disappeared with a crack. Duncan's flashlight hadn't rolled far.

Its feeble light was reflected by an old, splintered mirror.

Chapter 11: Promise

Duncan wasn't in the building.

Shay already knew he wouldn't be, but some part of her still hoped until the last radio call came in. It was only confirmation he wasn't hanging out in the parking lot.

Everyone else was talking loudly, but the words didn't hold any weight, sliding around her like water droplets down a windshield. The last thing to really sink in had been Max and Gideon holding her back from doing something drastic to the mirror.

She slumped in her seat. They'd moved her back to base, where Max insisted it was safe, but she had no idea if that was true. If it was, how could she live with herself? If she hadn't gone to change the battery, Duncan and Gideon would have returned to base. He would still be there. He would still be safe.

"Hey." Max sat next to her and handed her a cup. She took it without questioning it. "I made it how you like it."

"You always do." Her voice sounded flat to her, but far away. Like someone else was speaking. She could feel the warmth and smell the coffee. It had enough creamer that it was milky pale. She forced her fingers around the Styrofoam. Her right hand still had trouble uncurling, her fingers blue and freezing from the ghost. Max had already looked them over and said they would probably be okay. She didn't know how they knew that, but she didn't question it.

"I still don't understand what happened." Vic looked older. His gray hair escaped from his bun. "Where did he go?"

"I don't know," Gideon repeated, for probably the fiftieth time. Shay was glad he wasn't telling them the truth, though she wasn't sure why. Maybe he hadn't seen what actually happened. "I looked away for a minute and he was just gone. I was worried he fell beneath the stage or something, but…"

He shrugged helplessly.

"He said he had a headache, maybe he just went home," Meri suggested.

Taylor frowned, her perfectly plucked eyebrows coming together, pulling a strand of her long, chestnut hair over her shoulder to twirl it around her fingers. Her purple nail polish flashed in the light. "His car is still here, though. And nothing around here is open this time of night. What about the video? We have to give the library something, don't we?"

"I can edit what we got, don't worry," Sam assured her.

Shay wanted to shake the lot of them until their teeth rattled. Her brother was possessed and missing, and they were worried about their stupid ghost hunting video. Reminding herself that they didn't know the whole story didn't help at all.

"Thanks, Sam," Gideon said. "I think we need to recuperate and then regroup. Maybe he'll show up in the meantime, or someone will hear from him."

"That's a good idea." Vic nodded. "Everyone head home, be safe, charge your phones. Maybe he texted us already."

Their phones were dead, even Shay's where it had been sitting back at base.

"I'll go with Shay and Max," Gideon offered. "That way they have a line to us, and I can make sure you two get home safely?"

"Sounds great," Vic said, without their consent.

"If that's okay with you, of course." Gideon looked at them expectantly.

"Yeah, it's fine," Max said. "We'll go back to my place, see if we hear anything."

Shay shrugged. They couldn't do anything else there. The mirror was broken. She had no idea where it went or how it worked. For all she knew Duncan, and whoever was currently in the driver's seat, was sitting back at the apartment.

"Do you want me to go with you?" Taylor asked.

"No, it's okay," Gideon said. "I've got it."

"If you're sure." Taylor smiled a bit. "Call me, okay? When you all get settled in."

Gideon nodded. "Of course. You, too. I'm sure he's fine."

"Absolutely, but deepest apologies this didn't turn out," Vic said. "Next time will be better, Max, I promise."

"Yeah, okay." Max put an arm around Shay's shoulders. It probably looked comforting to anyone else. To Gideon like they were trying to keep her warm. She knew they were keeping her from going for someone's throat. They'd always been the smart one.

Everyone said their goodbyes. Shay wasn't really listening. She let Max steer her to the parking lot. The building felt hollow. Like anything that had been lurking in its walls was gone. Whether it was in the mirror, or to wherever ghosts went when they weren't possessing people and trying to claw her face off, she couldn't say.

They got back to the car and crawled in the back seat. The front wasn't great, but in the back the pizza smell was stronger. Sometimes she swore there was a box lurking under the seat. At least she could be close to Max. Being curled up against them was about the only thing keeping her together.

Max plugged their phone in. The second it was working again they checked their texts and grimaced. "I have like. Fifty messages from Jo."

"Aww she likes you," Shay said. It was the first time she'd really spoken since the mirror. Somehow it felt like a betrayal.

"No, she's worried. I'll call her." Before they could their phone rang, Jo's empty contact image flooding the screen. "Wow. She really is psychic."

"Just answer the phone."

"Right. Hey, Jo, I—"

"What happened." Even over the tinny speaker Jo's tone brooked absolutely no nonsense.

"There was a mirror," Max said.

"I knew it!" Jo yelled. There was a crashing sound, followed by some mumbled cursing. "Sorry, nothing important. Is Shay okay?"

"Yes," Shay said. Mostly so Jo would know she was listening. "And no. Duncan, my brother, he's possessed."

"What?"

"And he went through the mirror, and it broke, and I don't know how that works or what's— " Her voice caught in her throat.

"We're heading your way, we can explain everything when we get there," Max said.

Jo sighed. "Okay. Okay yes, that's the best plan. I'll see you soon."

"Thanks, Jo," Max said, hanging up on her.

Gideon tapped on Max's window and they both jumped, turning to look at him with wide eyes. He opened the door. "Sorry. I have your backpack. You're going to have to drive, I came in the van."

"Can you drive stick?" Max asked.

"Yes?"

"Great." They fished their keys out and handed them over. "I'll give you directions. We're going to a friend's place."

"Are you guys going to explain anything?" Gideon asked. "At least a little bit? You know you just met me, right? I could drive you anywhere. I won't, but I just want you to be aware of that."

"You ignore my instructions and I'll kick you through the windshield," Max said, their voice surprisingly even.

"Max, that's so violent," Shay said.

Max rubbed her shoulder. "I will be violent for you."

"Aww."

Max gave her a bit of a squeeze and she felt a little warmer.

"Right." Gideon didn't seem put off by threats of potential death by windshield. He got in the front seat and started the car. It roared to life before the engine calmed to a steady growl. "Sorry."

"It's what it does, it's fine," Max said.

Max sat close for the entire drive, until the cold dissipated and Shay started to feel like a person again. She dozed, lulled by the drone of Max's voice, so close she could feel the vibration. It was steadier than the rumble of the car.

She jerked awake when they pulled to a stop.

"Spellbound?" Gideon glanced back at them.

"Our friend owns it," Max said. Shay supposed Jo counted as a friend. They'd had sandwiches and tea together. "She knows about this stuff, so, she can explain things? I hope."

"Oh well. Okay," Gideon said. "I guess."

They got out of the car. Max adjusted her glasses for her and gave her a hand out the door. She felt like she could walk on her own, but she let them help her to the steps anyway. She was tired, but she wasn't nearly as cold. When she looked at her hands. Even in the dim light of the streetlamps, they seemed decidedly less blue.

The shop was dark, but Jo met them at the door. She'd swapped her jeans and boots for yoga pants and a pair of the fluffiest slippers Shay had ever seen. Her mass of purple hair was pulled back in a messy bun.

"You look exhausted," Jo told her. "Come on, I'll put on tea. I don't believe we've met…?"

"Gideon," he said. Shay hadn't even been aware he'd followed them to the door. "A friend, and a… witness? I guess?"

"He's a ghost hunter," Max said.

"Good." Jo nodded. "I'm Jo, nice to meet you. All of you, inside. Kitchen."

The kitchen was like a sea of light in the darkness. Shay sat down, not letting Max help her. She pretended to not notice when they scooted their chair closer to hers. Jo, in the least shocking event of the night, poured everyone a cup of tea. Shay's cup was more delicate than the one she'd used that afternoon, with little lilacs painted on it. The tea smelled like flowers. It tasted the way fresh cut hay smelled and she felt her shoulders relaxing. She had to pick it up with her left hand. Her right hand was still out of commission. It should have scared her, but it just felt like one more thing.

"What happened?" Jo asked.

Shay explained, in halting starts and faltering backtracks, but she managed to get the whole story out. It felt like it was being drawn from her bones, every bit of strength she had left going with it. "My plan is to find Duncan and punch the ghost out of him."

"I don't know if that will work," Jo said, tapping the pen she'd grabbed to take notes against her lips.

"Okay, I'm sorry, this is all incredibly crazy and I am not clear on who you are in all of this?" Gideon asked. "Clearly you know something but I'm in the dark here, and I do not like it."

"Let's start with I'm a witch." Jo looked at him like she was judging him and expecting failure.

"Seriously?" Gideon sounded skeptical. She rose a single eyebrow at him. He sighed and nodded. "I mean ghosts are one thing, but witches…what's next, a unicorn?"

"A unicorn?" Shay asked.

"Unicorns are cool." He shrugged. "Horses are terrifying and unicorns are like…uber horses. With stabbing."

"You've convinced me," she said. "Unicorns are cool."

"My coworker went missing a few days ago. He's the one that deals with haunted houses. I think it's tied to the mirrors and the ghosts. They should not be nearly this powerful," Jo said. "Shay has ghost touch, but she should be able to walk through a haunted building and at most get a few marks not…not almost killed every time she encounters a spirit. What about that sachet I made for you?"

Shay dug it out from under her collar. The green velvet was dark in places like it had been scorched. She opened it and tipped the contents into her hand. The herbs were just ash, and the rocks were blackened and cracked.

"Well." Jo frowned at it. "That's new. Oh, no, I'm out of my depth here. Let me um. Let me just get something for you to put that in."

She grabbed a jar from one of the shelves and Shay dusted her hand off into it. Jo sealed the jar and put it back on the shelf.

"That looked bad. Was that bad?" Max asked.

"Yes," Jo said. She sounded nearly as tired as Shay felt. "It explains some things. I was cleaning up from my reading and a mirror I use for scrying shattered. I knew something had probably gone wrong with you guys, and you weren't answering your phones. I was about to go there myself. Even my readings were off tonight. I was picking up details I shouldn't, missing things that were obvious. Something is very, very wrong."

"There's nothing we can do tonight," Max said. "Is it okay if I stay here?"

"Of course," Jo said. "I'd feel better if you all stayed, honestly. Arlo and I warded the house, it's as safe as we're going to get. We have a guest room and I can put fresh sheets on Arlo's bed? Or someone can take the couch."

"We can share the guest room," Max said.

"And I can take the couch," Gideon offered. "I mean, thank you so much for the hospitality, I don't want to put you out at all, but I do feel better staying here? Man, I have a lot of things to think about. I'm sorry about your brother, Shay. I know I already said that, but I am. We'll get him back."

"We?" Shay gave him a look. "You're going to help?"

"I mean, I have this." Gideon pulled a camera out of Max's backpack. "I filmed the whole thing, maybe I can figure something out. I'm not a witch, and I don't have whatever you have going for you, but I'm not running away just because I'm scared. Duncan was under my watch. I should have done more."

"I mean, I'm the one with ghost powers," Shay said. "And he's my brother."

"Yeah, so I'll help you get him back," Gideon said.

"Glad to have you on board," Jo said. Shay supposed she was in charge. "Come on, I'll get you all set up."

Shay grabbed Gideon's sleeve. "Hey um. Thank you. You know you don't have to do this."

"I know," Gideon said.

Jo led them through a darkened living room and a hall to an unassuming room with dark furniture and a bed covered in a faded purple and green quilt big enough for both of them. She insisted that Shay take a shower, saying she'd feel better and providing her with a huge t-shirt that must have belonged to Arlo for pajamas, since all of hers needed to be washed. It had a picture of an avocado and a piece of toast holding hands.

At least she had a pair of sweatpants shoved in the bottom of her bag.

Admittedly, the shower banished the last of the cold and she could move her fingers again.

It gave her too much time to really think.

She'd been worried Duncan had some sort of abilities. She still wasn't sure that he did, but he must have, if the ghost bypassed her and Gideon to possess him.

If she said something, he wouldn't have believed her. There was still the possibility it would have changed things. If only she'd just been a little braver. The maybes gnawed at her. Fear knotted up in her chest and she cried under the shower stream for a little longer than she would ever admit.

When she came back into the room Max was hunched over their phone. They looked up and a worried line appeared between their eyebrows. "Shay?"

"I'm all right." She sat next to them. "I really smell like lavender now, because that's all Jo has I guess, but I know you're fine with that."

Max turned and sniffed. "Wow, yeah. It's not bad, but you are very lavender-y."

"Creep." She shoved their shoulder slightly. "It is bad. I smell like I hate moths."

"I mean, that's fair."

"Moths are cool. And adorable."

"Mothman is cool. Moths are out to take over the world with their big, dusty wings. Mind control spores." Max gave her a concerned look. "You sure you're-"

"Please don't ask." She uncurled her hands. They still hurt, but not nearly as badly. The blue and purple marks were fading, slowly. "See? All good."

"Good." Max clearly didn't believe her. "Sorry to say, nothing from Duncan, not even on your phone. And no activity on any of his accounts."

They showed her their phone. The last thing on Duncan's feed was a selfie of him and Gideon with the caption "*hunting for ghosts with Gid! #PEIRS #ghosthunting*" It made her chest feel tight and heavy all over again and she looked back down at her knees.

"Hey. We're going to get him back." Max put an arm around her and she leaned against their shoulder. "I promise."

"Yeah." She smiled, a little bit. Max always did keep their promises.

Chapter 12: The Blue Hour

Shay woke with a start.

Nightmares of mirrors that spilled skulls like the eyes of terrible gods, weeping tears of human lament, clung to her like cobwebs. She lay in bed, staring at an unfamiliar ceiling. Max breathed gently next to her.

The room was dark. Cobalt sky peered in through a gap in the curtains. Her mom always said the blue hour was the best time of day, especially in the morning, when everything was quiet and the world hadn't started yet.

She wasn't the kind of tired that lent itself to sleep, so she swung her legs out of bed. She shoved her feet into a pair of slippers Jo had pressed on her the night before, saying something about hardwood floors and the cold, along with a thick bathrobe that Shay was happy to pull on.

She leaned her elbows on the wide windowsill. It was too dark to really see anything except the black cut out of trees against the sky and the domes of honey colored light under streetlamps. The sky was already too bright for stars, but the crescent moon hung just at the edge of her view, small and silver.

She shivered and shrugged more effectively into her borrowed bathrobe. She put a hand near the radiator under the window. The warmth coming off it didn't reach her.

Frost crept up the outside of the window.

She saw the mist before anything else, flowing across the ground.

The ghosts came next, streaming between houses and shops, giving Spellbound a wide berth. They glided forward like they were floating on the fog. Large skirts and top hats mingled with jeans and hoodies.

She glanced back at Max, but they just murmured something in their sleep and turned over, taking the blanket with them.

When she looked back someone was staring at her.

She lurched back, barely stifling a noise of surprise. The ghost had holes where its eyes should have been. The gaping darkness loomed behind it.

It passed away from the window, towards the kitchen. She followed it, into the hall and into the minuscule living room.

Light seeped around the edges of the kitchen door. She slipped inside, trying to keep too much light from waking up the lump on the couch that was Gideon.

"Oh, good morning." Jo was sitting at the table. It was clear she hadn't slept much. She had bags under her eyes and her hair was still in a bun, strands falling loose around her face. She looked less put together without makeup, and younger than Shay had thought.

"Yeah, it's morning." Shay walked past her to the windows, yanking back the curtains. The ghost with holes for eyes had already moved on, but she could see the others. A ghastly parade drifting across the street, through dark houses and shops. "And there's about fifty ghosts outside."

She wasn't sure on the number, but it felt like a lot.

"What?" Jo stood up, moving to the window. She shivered and pulled her cardigan closer.

They stood there in silence as the blue began to pale and the first sunlight shone over the mountain, gilding the tops of trees. The mist rolled on, taking the ghosts with it to some unknown destination.

"I saw a little movement," Jo admitted. Shay almost jumped. "And flickers of things. Shadows. Do you still see them?"

"No." Shay said. "They were just floating along. All in the same direction."

She pointed across the street.

"Hm." Jo folded her arms. "Maybe you were witnessing some sort of crossing on event, having to do with sunrise. That seems…I don't know, astrologically potent enough? I've never heard of anything like it."

"Yeah, well, I guess I'm not waking up early anymore, if that's the case," Shay said.

"That's fair," Jo said, still frowning like she was trying to piece together a puzzle and couldn't find a corner piece. "You look better."

"Thanks?" Shay shrugged. "I feel better, I guess all it took was a hot shower and some sleep."

"Oh! I washed your clothes." Jo motioned her to follow. The laundry room was tucked in by the back door. There were no ghosts outside. Shay checked.

She felt a little better once she was dressed in actual clothes. The smell of coffee hit her when she walked back into the kitchen. She felt her shoulders relaxing. She'd been worried she would have to drink more tea. She was pretty sure if she tried she would burst.

"Hey." Jo was at the table again like a thousand ghosts hadn't just passed by the window. Then again, she hadn't seen them. The curtains were open, letting in the pale morning light.

"I'm trying to figure out if there are any other mirrors out there."

"Yeah?" Shay poured herself a cup of coffee and fished some creamer out of the fridge. "If there are, what do we do? Could we use them to find Duncan?"

"Potentially. We could investigate?" Jo suggested. She sighed, shoving hair out of her face. "I don't know. I wish Arlo was here, he'd know what to do. All I can think is we need to get our hands on one of those mirrors. Properly warded, I might even be able to track this all down to its source, which I imagine will help us find your brother. But, and I hate to say this, I really don't think I can do it without you."

"What do you mean?" Shay asked.

"Well, I have a few ideas," Jo said. "We need to stop by your place and get something of your brother's, I can use it to track him down, unless you're carrying something of his…?"

"No, that would be weird," Shay said. "Wait, I have a shirt of his in my bag. No, I left that at Max's. And I wore it like the last four times so it's not his anymore."

"Right." Jo nodded. "I'll need help with that. And I can't see ghosts well. Not nearly as well as you. I can sense them, but it's not the same. If you can point me to the mirror, I can find your brother. Probably. I don't want to promise anything but…"

"It's a start." Shay nodded, trying to not hope too much. Something that felt more like anxiety bubbled up inside of her. "What do we do when we find him? What if he's still possessed?

"I hope that's not the case. If it is, I might be able to do something. I'm sorry. I wish I was more useful." Jo sighed. "As it is, I think I've found all of the places that have most likely had a mirror in them."

Shay sat next to her and Jo slid her tablet so it was between them. There was a map of the valley, with purple stars drawn in a rough crescent. "Arlo was called to an old school and found a mirror inside, right here. It was broken by the time he got there. This is the house you and Max investigated. Here's the theater, and an old laundromat that I heard of. I wish I knew where Arlo was called to… Anyway. It seems to be making a circle, so I think we'll find our next mirror around here."

She indicated the spot on the map that there were no marks at all.

"That makes as much sense as anything else," Shay said. "Why a circle?"

"Spiritually it could be significant," Jo said. "If I'm right then the center is here, in downtown. There are a lot of hauntings there, lots of bad energy. It's not the healthiest of places."

"Probably why nothing stays open," Shay said.

"That's exactly it. Whatever is targeting it, well, it can't be good. I looked through a bunch of forums, social media, everywhere I could think of. There's been a rash of ghost sightings in this area," Jo continued. "Bonus, we have a job there. Well, Arlo has a job, but I'll just have to do it and hope for the best. The only other thing I can think of is going back to the house you and Max went to-"

"We could stop by there first?" Shay suggested. "I think they still have the key."

"Good, go ask them," Jo said. "I'll make breakfast and we can figure things out."

"What about the ghosts this morning?" Shay asked. "They were all heading in the same direction, that's weird. What way is that, anyway?"

"It's south." Jo frowned. "That's…towards downtown."

"Coincidence?" Shay asked.

"Right now? I'm not putting any faith in coincidence. We can check that out, too." Jo looked even more frazzled. "I'll wake Gideon up, you get Max."

"Okay." She realized that Jo was putting a lot of time and effort into helping her, and she was missing someone, too. She couldn't imagine Duncan being gone for longer than he already had been. She was worried to the point of being sick. "Thanks, Jo. You've been a huge help and you barely know me. We'll find Arlo, too, I'm sure."

"Thank you for saying that," Jo said. She didn't sound like she believed Shay, but she looked grateful all the same. "I'm not just doing this because…but if you would I'd be grateful…"

"I bet it's all connected," Shay said. "And if not, I promise. I'm going to help."

"Thank you." Jo looked like she wanted to say more, but she just patted Shay's shoulder as she passed by.

Shay made up another coffee and took both mugs back to the room. Gideon had turned to face the back of the couch.

Max was sitting up and blinking sleepily at her. Their hair was a mess, framing their face and softening the angles.

"You left," they said.

"I left." Shay held out their mug. "For coffee. I figured you'd forgive me."

"It is so early, Shay. But I do forgive you." They accepted the drink.

"How generous." Shay set her own coffee down on the nightstand. "I don't think Jo slept, she was doing things with maps, but we may have a lead. Do you still have the key to the Johnson house?"

"Yeah, haven't had a chance to return it," Max said. "Why?"

"She thinks if we find one of the not-broken mirrors she can use it to 'trace it back to its source', or something," Shay said. "That maybe we can use it to find Duncan? Before whatever has him finds us, anyway. I think. He said he would see me later. Well, whatever possessed him did. I don't know.

She was talking about scrying and a lot about Arlo and I'm no good with. Things."

She sighed and flopped face down on the bed.

Max reached over and tried to comb through her tangled hair with their fingers. Usually she braided it at night, but they'd both been too tired. It probably looked like a family of rats had a long-term lease.

"I could ask Leela if she'll give you a haircut," Max offered.

"Does she do everything?" Shay asked.

"Pretty much," Max admitted. "You'd rock an undercut."

"I'd look like a tiny round Duncan, no thanks." She turned her head to the side so she could breathe and looked up at them, even though they were blurry with her glasses knocked askew. "Sorry."

"For what?" They kept trying with her hair.

"For…I dunno. Messing stuff up. Being bad at life." She turned her face back to the blankets so her voice was muffled. This was probably the type of conversation she should have had sitting up, like an adult, but maybe she hadn't ever grown up in any of the ways that mattered.

There were moments, more than she cared to think about, where she felt frozen in time. She'd gone to school, sure, but all she'd managed to do was get her generals done. She still didn't know what she wanted to do. Her GPA hadn't been stellar and she still didn't have a job. Sometimes she didn't think she even wanted a job.

She was stuck. Still the awkward teenager in the summer before college, hating what was behind her and terrified of what was ahead.

"You haven't done either of those things," Max sounded confused and a little concerned. "Where is this coming from, Shay? Is it about Duncan? That's not your fault. We're going to get him back. It's going to be okay."

"It's everything." Shay propped herself up on her elbows. "There's all of this happening, and I just trip into it and put everyone else in danger. I feel like…I should be able to do something, but I just miss, I guess. I'm always missing things."

"I don't think I could do any better," Max said. "It's not your job to keep everyone safe. It's the opposite, we should be helping you."

"Mm." She rolled onto her back and held up her hands. There were still blue marks on her fingers. "Maybe."

"I shouldn't have gone off to that dressing room," they admitted, quietly. "This is my fault, actually. I said I'd keep you safe, but I took a camera and went off. I'm sorry, Shay. If I'd been there, you wouldn't have gone to change the battery…"

"What? No, Max, this is entirely not your fault, you aren't my keeper," Shay said. She wondered if they'd felt the same way the night before, and she'd been too self-absorbed to notice. "Or Duncan's."

Max sighed. "Well. If you say so."

"I do say so and I'm right," she said. "Besides, if you had gone to change the battery, that ghost would have just snagged Duncan and no one would have seen what happened. So. It's…well, it's bad, but…"

"No, I get it." They adjusted her glasses for her. "We just have to do better."

"Yeah." Shay supposed that was all they could do. "By the way, there were like, a million ghosts outside this morning, and you slept through it."

Max's expression was comically dismayed.

"I mean, to be fair, Jo barely saw them-"

"No, I…I mean that's wild, but I grabbed my keys and it's gone." Max held up their keychain.

"Wait, you don't mean…"

They nodded. "The key to the Johnson house. It's gone."

CHAPTER 13:
MIRROR GHOST

"Heading to a bar at nine in the morning. We've really hit rock bottom."

Shay thought Gideon's joke fell a little flat, but was too nice to say so. Max managed a weak chuckle.

World Tree Bar and Restaurant, their current destination, had opened the year before, taking over an abandoned warehouse in downtown Ainsley. It had been the place to go for a hot minute, but Shay had never actually gone, even though Ainsley was only half an hour's drive away from Teton Falls, in the opposite direction of Doveton.

"It's the closest potential site that we've had a call from," Jo said, not looking up from her tablet.

"I know," Gideon said. He was sitting in the back with Shay. It was cold, the heat blasting from the front trickling to the back of the Explorer. Shay didn't normally sit in the back. She wasn't enjoying it.

"You sure you want to come?" Shay asked. "If there's a mirror, there's probably a powerful ghost."

"Already said I'd help. Besides, you literally punched a ghost out of existence. I am sticking with you." Gideon grinned at her.

"Technically that was more the sachet than me, I just stuck it in there," Shay said, but she couldn't help smiling back.

"Right, sure." Gideon nodded. "Still sticking with you. So, what do you typically do for a job like this? How does a bookstore owner end up doing house calls? I'm genuinely curious."

"It is a metaphysical bookstore," Max said.

"Still."

"Well, the vast majority of spirits are site bound, so our clients can't exactly bring the haunting to us," Jo said. "It's actually how Arlo and I got started. I was doing tarot readings online as a side hustle and he needed help with a house cleansing. Since I was in the area I agreed to meet him. We started working together after that, and when my grandma left me the house I decided to open up the shop. Have an official place to do readings and a home base for everything else."

"And a place for random people you meet who can touch ghosts," Shay said.

"Yes, that too." Jo shrugged. She sounded a bit fragile. Shay couldn't blame her. Without Max she'd probably fall to pieces. "Typically, this would be Arlo's job. He would go in, get a feel for the place, try to follow the energy. He would then either remove the object that was causing the haunting, or he would instruct the owner on how to cleanse the area or keep things quiet. If needed I would see the place, too. I'm hoping to find one of those mirrors, especially since we no longer have ah… legal access to the other one. Barring that, well, I'll just have to do what Arlo would and try to figure out the haunting."

"Renovations or a new object in the bar," Gideon said.

"Yes, precisely."

Max chimed in. "Or something could have happened recently that made things worse."

"Or satanic cult symbols," Shay offered.

Gideon shrugged. "Those are largely myths. Especially around here. We have a whole different cult flavor. Mostly doomsday stuff."

"If there is a symbol, which is unlikely, it would probably be tied to Halloween decorations. But despite what you may have seen on tv, that usually doesn't cause any sort of activity," Jo said. "Or at least nothing noticeable to the average person."

Shay thought for a moment. "Say there are satanic or whatever flavor cults making ghosts happen. How would you go about joining one? Do they approach you? Do you have to know someone? Maybe you can look it up on the internet."

"Shay, don't you dare," Max said.

Which was really the only encouragement she needed. "Too late. I'm looking it up. Right now. We're going to get arrested any second now for googling forbidden knowledge."

"Shay! I mean it! Don't!"

Being in the back seat did have his advantages. She'd pouted when Max offered Jo shotgun and the aux cord, but now they couldn't reach her and she could do whatever she wanted.

"What did you find out?" Gideon looked interested.

"All right. Here we go. Cults are a thing and they're bad, but satanic cults? Not so much," Shay said. "Largely an urban legend thing. So, we're probably safe from a group of people wearing black robes and sacrificing goats."

Max exhaled loudly through their nose. "Why?"

"With everything going on I thought maybe it could be a ghost cult. Causing all of the commotion. Cultmotion."

"I meant why goats?"

"Oh!" She shrugged. "I dunno. Goats are like proto-demons. All the horns, headbutting, screaming…you get the idea."

"That makes sense," Max agreed.

"Not really," Gideon said.

"Not at all." Jo shook her head.

Shay grinned. "Hell is Goatopia."

At least Max laughed at her terrible joke, though she was pretty sure Gideon was trying very hard not to smile. The atmosphere of the car felt a little less strained, at least.

"Yes, yes, hilarious," Jo said in a way that clearly meant she didn't think it was funny at all. "If you two are done, we're laying down some ground rules. We're going in teams of two. Gideon and I will be team one, you two will be the other."

"Aww, buddy system with my bestie," Shay said. "Sorry, Gideon."

"It's so we have someone who is more supernaturally inclined on each team, and someone with a camera," Jo explained. Max had their phone, which she could point out they all had one, but decided not to. Jo was the expert. "We're not going to have a very big window of time to investigate so we have to make everything count. If you see anything weird, text me or move to my position immediately. We'll all have sachets in our pockets and bags."

Shay had a necklace, too. Another small sachet that Jo had made up for her. Hopefully this one wouldn't turn to ash.

"I'm going to introduce you three as my associates," Jo said. "Please try to remain as professional as you can."

Shay knew that was directed at her. She sat up straight and nodded when she saw Jo's eyes flick to the rearview mirror.

"If this works out, maybe you can hire me for real," Shay said. It wasn't like she had any other prospects knocking down her door, and if she had to move into Jo's guest room she might as well work for her keep.

"Maybe," Jo said.

"Then I can work off my probably increasing debt to you," Shay said.

"Oh, you will definitely be doing that." Jo looked over her shoulder to grin at her. "You've racked up quite the bill, between advice, the materials for the sachets, my valuable time…"

"Yes, yes, I get it, I'm indebted to you forever." Shay didn't really want to think about that. Any money she'd managed to save while in college was hemorrhaging from her bank account. "I can sit behind a counter and ring people up and all that."

"I'm good," Max said. "I mean, I'll be over all the time anyway, but the daycare is enough for me."

"I don't want a job," Gideon said.

"What do you do?" Shay asked.

"Graphic design, I freelance," he said. "That's why I have so much time for this little side hobby."

"Did you design the P.E.I.R.S. logo?" Shay asked. He nodded. "Yes. I knew it. I love it. This is my new favorite shirt."

"Well that is a pretty high compliment, thank you." He grinned, obviously pleased. "Want a sticker, too?"

He held up his camera. It had a vinyl sticker of the logo.

"Oh, heck yes. I dunno where I'll put it, but I definitely want it," Shay said. Gideon laughed.

Maybe if nothing worked out with Jo she could freelance seeing ghosts. She wasn't exactly sure how much that particular skill would be needed outside of ghost hunting groups. Though it was enough that Jo and Arlo had built a business on house calls, in Teton Falls of all places, so maybe it wasn't the wildest idea she'd ever had.

It didn't matter. What mattered was finding Duncan. Then she would worry about everything else.

They pulled into a nearly empty parking lot. The bar was a tall, brick building. "World Tree" was done in wrought iron, copper and bronze branches and leaves spreading behind it. It would have looked classy if a whole ton of neon didn't scrawl out types of beer below it, the tubing dull in the morning light. The windows were dark.

Max parked the car and they got out. Their breath plumed in white clouds in the frigid air.

Jo strode to the door and knocked on it. A moment later a tall, curvy woman answered. Her dark hair spiked and jagged where it wasn't buzzed short. She was wearing a tank top and ripped jeans despite the cold, displaying tattoos done in dark ink on her olive skin. The smudges around her eyes were half exhaustion and half eyeliner, her lips had the colorless look of someone who had rubbed their lipstick off.

"Hey, good to see you." She gave Jo a smile that transformed her face from neutral to something bright and soft. "Thanks for coming. These the people you talked about?"

"My associates, yes. This is Shay, Max, and Gideon. This is Morgan." Jo gestured between them, like her fingers were itching to put a kettle on.

"Nice to meet ya." Morgan graced them with a slightly less brilliant smile. Shay was a little smitten, anyway. "Come on in."

The interior was dim and barely warmer than it was outside. Right inside the door the tree that the entire restaurant must have been named for was visible. It spread above the floor and over an old, grated metal catwalk above their heads. Crystal baubles hung from the branches. With the myriad of lights on it probably looked like magic.

The lights weren't even on, but it was still whimsical.

A bar wrapped around one side of the room, lined with stools. Tables filled half of the floor, their chairs upside down on top of them, legs up like dead spiders. The rest must have been a dance floor with a small, raised stage at the other end. For the moment it was empty.

There was something eerie and melancholy about the empty bar. Light streamed through the highest windows, but didn't really reach the floor below. Only a few buzzing lights cut through the gloom.

"We've been kind of having problems all over, the last week or so. It's been getting worse, so I called Jo," Morgan started her explanation. "She used to do readings for me, back in the day, and I knew she had that new business…anyway, there was a live band performing. We do it every Friday night, but this time something shoved a speaker off of the stage. It was one of those big ones, too, not some tiny Bluetooth crap being tossed around. Probably about as big as you."

She indicated Shay.

"There was a bunch of weird feedback before that, too. Sometimes the tree shakes, like there's a lot of wind, but no one feels anything. People say they feel like a snake is slithering against their ankle or arm but there's nothing there. I've felt it, it's not fun. Really cold. Glasses fly off of the tables. The other day one of the bottles just shattered."

She motioned to the bar. There was an array of bottles lining the shelves, but if one of them was conspicuously missing, Shay wouldn't know.

"Let's see…" Morgan chewed her bottom lip a bit. "People have been seeing weird faces in the women's bathroom mirror. Sometimes when I'm closing up I hear dragging noises on the catwalk but nothing's ever up there. I dunno. We've always had weird stuff happening, but lately it's so much worse."

Shay had been listening attentively, but she practically leaned forward when Morgan mentioned the mirror. That definitely sounded like something they needed to check out.

"Okay." Max had been recording her on their phone, Shay realized a moment too late. "That's a lot. Lots of great detail, too. Anything else?"

"I dunno, cold spots I guess." Morgan shrugged. Shay looked at her bare shoulders and wondered how cold it had to be for her to notice. "But it could be drafts, it's an old building."

"I definitely feel a presence here." Jo glanced at the bar. Shay looked, too, but didn't see anything, not even a wisp of fog. "Shay? How about you?"

"Nothing yet," she said. "At least nothing I can see. It does feel like something."

She wasn't sure how to tell Jo that the bar felt like the Johnson house. It might not have had anything to do with ghosts at all. It just felt empty, even with the furniture and the tree. Like something had sucked the life out of it. Without the crowds to drink and dance, the bar was just an empty building with a pretty tree.

"Okay, we'll look around," Jo said. "Gideon and I will take the stage. Shay, Max, you check the bathroom."

"Sounds good." Max put their phone away. "I need to take my contacts out, anyway."

"I'll be here." Morgan sat on one of the stools, looking a little deflated. Shay wasn't sure if it was from work or from the ghosts.

Maybe both. In college, Shay had worked at the front desk of the gym. A dog, not even a particularly well trained one, could have easily done her job and she still went home absolutely exhausted every day.

They headed into the hallway with a restroom sign over it.

"So, nothing yet?" Max asked.

"Nada," she said. "Some of the stuff she said sounds like a legitimate haunting, right? A bad one. A good one? Semantics. Anyway, the slither thing could be a creep and the glasses and stuff could just be, y'know, drunk people things. It is a bar."

"You've been to one bar," Max said.

"Well, it sort of made a lasting impression," Shay said. She'd turned twenty-one just before leaving college, and her roommate insisted that they go out. The roommate proceeded to get completely trashed in the first bar they went to. They had to take an Uber home, and her roommate had left right after that for some party or another.

It hadn't been the best birthday ever. For Max's twenty-first she'd just bought them a beer from the grocery store. They'd hated it.

"Yeah, your crappy birthday." Max patted her shoulder.

"Eh, I lived." She shrugged. "Besides, any birthday without you is bound to be crappy. I expect the best party next year."

"You got it." Max smiled.

The hallway was painted black, making it seem darker than it really was. The doors to the bathrooms were dark wood. She opened the one that had a copper sign with a tree and the letter W made of its branches.

"I kind of thought that a bar called 'World Tree' that employs a probable lesbian would be a little more bathroom inclusive." Max looked over at the other bathroom with its "M" sign.

"M is for Max," Shay said. "W is for Welcome, Max. I'd pick the more welcoming one, men's bathrooms are disgusting."

"Oh, agreed," Max said, following her into the bathroom. "Well. This sure is a bathroom."

The room was painted avocado green with burnished copper stall walls and a large mirror over a pair of sinks. The tree motif continued in the mirror frame, branches spreading across the top. They were really committed to their aesthetic. She peered into the mirror, determined that if there was anything, she would be the one to find it.

Shay wasn't surprised by how pale and tired she looked in the mirror. Max was washed out, too, but judging by their actual face it was mostly due to the bad lighting.

"I look really bad." She leaned over the sinks to look in the mirror, her braid falling over her shoulder.

"You don't," Max said, automatically.

"Shut up and put your face next to mine, I wanna see something."

"No," Max said.

"Max. Just do it." Shay grabbed their hoodie strings and pulled them down to her level. Despite looking as flawless as ever, in the mirror their skin was sallow and the bags under their eyes were dark and heavy. "Yeah. Okay. Maybe someone just saw their own face in this mirror, because yikes."

"Can I take out my contacts, please?" Max asked. "I'm getting a headache."

"I'm sorry." Shay let go of their hoodie. "Go on, yank your eyeballs out, I'm sure I can amuse myself."

Max made a disgusted noise and thunked their bag on the counter. She ignored them, looking around.

Max waxing poetic about it being a bathroom was just about spot on. The stalls were clean of everything but some graffiti, mostly hearts with initials and a few phone numbers that promised a "good time". There was a bench made of dark wood, presumably for sitting, though she'd never seen anyone sitting on a bathroom bench before.

In the end the only thing that really seemed to stand out was the mirror. She drummed her fingers on the surface. "Hello? Ghosties? I'm looking for my brother. He was dragged through a mirror, so you can probably help me out!"

"Think that will work?" Max asked.

"You miss one hundred percent of the shots you don't take," Shay said.

"So, no." Max put on their glasses and pulled a face. "Ugh."

"Shut up, you look glorious," Shay said. "Except in this mirror. Which I hate."

"Tell me how you really feel." Max grinned at her using their reflection and she glared back the same way. "No, really, we're a little washed out, but it's not that bad. And I'd blame that on the lighting."

They pointed up at the strip lighting above the mirror that cast a sickly yellow glow.

"Well, maybe, but we look really sick," Shay said.

"Uh…" Max leaned forward and squinted. "I guess?"

"No, seriously, like you have bags under your eyes and your cheeks are sunken and…"

Max's reflection was sloughing off flesh in big flakes. She looked at them in horror, but the real Max looked perfectly healthy, if a little confused. When she turned back to their reflection all that remained was a skull.

"Y'know." She tapped the mirror again. Ripples of green light raced away from her fingers. "It would probably have worked better if they didn't have hair."

Mirror Max still had a full head of hair. It was even tucked into a headband. They were wearing glasses, too, despite the lack of nose and ears to hold the frames. The skull clattered its teeth at her before the bottom jaw unhinged and dropped out of sight.

"Don't you sass me, I'm giving you tips."

She wasn't sure how she was so calm. Maybe because the ghost was still clearly in the mirror, and technically just using their reflections.

"Haunted mirror?" Max asked. The skull lost all of its teeth, one by one.

"Super haunted." Shay leaned forward. "Okay, mirror ghost. I don't know if you have answers for me but since you're here let's chat, shall we? What's going on? Where's my brother?"

Shay looked at her own face as her flesh fell away, too, eyes streaming down her cheeks in thick, white tears. "Ew. That's not even scary. It's just gross."

Like Max, her skull was still wearing glasses and had her hair, pulled back in a messy braid. It was weird, seeing her own vertebrae twist and turn with her movements. She even opened and closed her mouth a few times, watching her jaw work without any visible ligaments.

"Okay, that's enough." She felt a little sick. "I'm not afraid of bad luck. You tell me where my brother is, or I'm going to smash you. Into a million pieces. Then where will you be? In a dump."

"Do you really think it knows?" Max asked. "It could be site bound. And smashing the mirror could release it."

"Don't tell it that," she whispered. "If it even tries to crawl out of there I'll smack it with so much anti-ghost salt it'll feel it forever. Besides, Duncan was taken into a mirror. It has it have some idea. And it's my only lead."

She hoped, anyway. At least the mirror wasn't turning black, like the previous ones. Maybe that only worked for really old mirrors. This one was practically brand new.

"C'mon, mirror ghost. Yell. Scream. Write it. I don't care how you communicate, just get on with it. Except American Sign Language because unfortunately I don't know that."

"I know some!" Max made a few gestures. "I told it my name is Max. Did it say anything?"

"No." She'd turned, a little, to watch Max, but the skull in the mirror kept staring straight ahead. "Okay, that's actually pretty good. Kudos."

The ghost lifted one hand, completely independent of what Shay was doing. The hair and glasses faded away, leaving behind a bare skull. It wrote on the inside of the mirror, almost painstakingly slow.

Hello Shay.

She jerked away from the mirror. The skeleton in the mirror, now taller than her, leaned its head slightly to one side, but didn't bother to try and copy her movements anymore. There was something around it, like with the first skeleton.

I know where your brother is.

"Yeah? Then tell me."

I will show you.

"What does that mean?" Shay asked. Fear felt like ice stabbing into her spine.

Your ride is here.

"What?"

The mirror cracked with a sound like a gunshot and her reflection returned to normal. She looked even paler than she had when they first walked in, her eyes wide.

"What happened?" Max asked. "Shay?"

A deep thrum filled the bar. The mirror rippled, the frame jangling.

"What was that?" Max's voice cracked and they grabbed her arm.

"I…" She could feel it, now. The chill in the air, the heaviness of it, how it seemed to settle right down into her. "I think that might be my ride."

Chapter 19: Wires

Shay hurried out of the bathroom.

Every other door in the hallway slammed shut. The lights flickered and died. The sullen red glow of the emergency exit washed over them.

"What do you mean, ride?" Max's voice had gone high and squeaky.

"Something the ghost said. We have to make sure everyone else got out." Shay checked her phone, but Jo hadn't tried to text or call.

Wind, sudden and terrifyingly strong, tried to shove her down the hallway into the main room. Fog rolled around her ankles, sucking the warmth out of the air. Shay ran back into the bar.

The sound was louder that time. It was so deep she felt it more than heard it. It resonated in the copper tree and sent it humming in response, its branches vibrating. The crystals and lights shook and clattered together. High above the windows rattled in their frames. Light no longer spilled from them, their surface dark.

Morgan and Jo were standing near the bar, looking up at the tree in trepidation. Gideon was recording.

"What are you doing?" She yelled at them. "Get out of here!"

"What?" Gideon turned the camera on her.

"Get! Out!"

The ghost pulled itself through the floor behind him.

It moved like stiff clockwork, all jerking motions and sudden shifts, yanking itself out of the cement. It wasn't even fully out and it already towered over Gideon.

Shay sprinted towards him. Gideon was turning, too slowly, like he was underwater.

She pushed him out of the way and something painfully cold wrapped tightly around her waist.

It heaved her up into the air. She screamed. Up and down lost all sense and meaning for a brief and sickening moment. The only sound was her own voice and the wind rushing in her ears.

A moment of weightlessness, her heavy stomach far below. The bar spread out beneath her, too small, and she knew she couldn't come back down safely.

She fell.

She hit the catwalk, hard enough that she bounced and hit the railing, sprawling out on the metal grating. She tried to breathe but the air wasn't hitting her lungs. She panicked for a moment before she could finally breathe, straining her probably bruised ribs.

"Shay!" Max was yelling. They'd probably been yelling for a while. "I'm coming! I'll be right there!"

She coughed, her entire left side protesting. An eternity later, or what felt like one, she managed to sit up. She used the railing to haul herself to her feet. Pain shot through her when she put weight on her left foot. Her ankle throbbed like it was on fire. She sagged against the bars.

Something slithered over the other end of the catwalk. She thought it was a snake for a brief moment.

It was a sleeve. Muted blue, too long and strangely flat. Something writhed under the fabric.

The ghost pulled itself in jarring spasms. It was even taller than she thought, thin like it had been stretched out. Even with its back hunched it still loomed over her. The sleeves and pant legs of the coveralls it was wearing were trailed out behind it.

It didn't have a face.

Where there should have been a head was just darkness, like a child scribbling with a black crayon. It moved and flowed like static.

She tried to take a step back and landed on her bad foot. She sat down with a clang.

It dropped to all fours. Its limbs bent in horrible, spidery ways. It scuttled towards her and she screamed again. The head elongated, the dark static stretching out.

Wires.

Hundreds and hundreds of wires, bending and twisting around and around each other.

A sleeve whipped forward and wrapped around her arm. She ripped at the icy fabric with her fingers, tearing it like soggy cardboard.

Underneath that thick cables coiled around her arm. They bent and twisted at odd angles under her touch.

More wires shot from its chest, wrapping around her. She tried to grab a sachet from her pocket, but more lines trapped her wrist against her.

The ghost pulled her closer, too close. She could feel the ice of it burning the side of her face.

It let out a sound like a massive guitar string being plucked.

Shay tried to cover her ears with her free hand, but the sound was in her chest, humming deep in her bones. The lights lining the catwalk flared to life, bright and brief, before exploding in showers of sparks. The baubles hanging from the tree popped and snapped. They dropped around her, pinging off of the grating and rails.

The sound cut off. The silence in its wake was almost more deafening. The hold on her loosened and she yanked back, scrambling away, not daring to turn around or try to get up.

The ghost whirled around. Max and Jo were standing at the end of the catwalk.

Jo held a white candle. The flame burned higher than it should have been able to. A halo of golden light surrounded Jo like she was some sort of avenging angel, the candle her sword, ready to smite down the ghost.

"Run!" Max yelled at her. They had a sachet in their hand. "Get downstairs!"

It lurched towards them. Shay pulled herself up by the railing. The bars were freezing under her hands. Jo held up a candle as the wires lashed out at her. They didn't reach her, slapping against an invisible barrier, sparking green and gold with the jangle of a smashed violin.

"Hurry, I can't hold it for long!" Jo yelled. Shay didn't want to leave them, but she didn't think she really had a choice. She limped as quickly as she could down the other side of the catwalk. Only the railing kept her upright.

She was halfway down the stairs when she saw the mirror.

It had been tucked underneath the stairs. It could have been an unused decoration if it weren't glowing. Fog flowed through the surface and across the floor.

Just like the mirror Duncan walked through.

Something touched her and she almost screamed before she realized it was Gideon.

"Sorry, here to help, didn't mean to scare you," he said.

"The mirror." She had to hope he understood. Maybe it wasn't a good idea, stepping into a mirror with no idea where she'd end up, but it was the only one she had.

"I-"

A sleeve shot out. It didn't touch him, but Gideon was knocked into the banister anyway. Shay whirled around. The ghost was right behind her. Max and Jo were running towards her, but as if in a dream they were moving far too slowly. They'd never reach her. Gideon was being shoved down the stairs by something even she couldn't see.

It was all her.

She screamed, right in the ghost's face. It was a wild, unbridled sound that ripped itself out of her throat. She punched it with everything she had, not caring that she didn't have a sachet in hand, not even worrying about her own safety.

It rippled and for a moment she thought she saw a face.

Jo threw something and its edges distorted, flickers of blue and green flame licking across its shoulders and trailing down its long, tattered sleeves.

Max ran through it and it burst into wisps of flame and smoke that she could almost smell.

"C'mon, Shay, I got you."

Max put an arm around her shoulders. Gideon was on her other side, helping them carry her down.

"Wait! No! The mirror!" Her throat hurt. All of her hurt. "There's a mirror! We have to-"

"It's coming back," Gideon said, glancing behind them.

"We gotta go," Max said.

"Through the mirror!" she insisted.

"No way," Max said. "We're not in any shape for that."

They hit the last stair and were shoved in different directions. Shay hit the floor, hard, and looked up to see the mirror. It was close enough the wind blowing through it rippled her hair.

"Ow," Max said.

"What was that?" Gideon was trying to sit up.

Wires shot out of the floor, wrapping around him and Max. They were both pulled down to the cement. Jo held up her candle. It didn't matter. She had to retreat up the stairs.

"Hey!" Shay stood up, shaky with nothing to support her. The mirror was right there. She could step into it.

She could find Duncan.

The mist rose up in a column from the floor, reforming the ghost. It let go of Max and Gideon, its wires returning to its sleeves. It hurtled towards her, sleeve wrapping around her arm and yanking it up, pulling them both towards the mirror.

She turned, ignoring the pain, ignoring how much she wanted to find her brother. She used the ghost's momentum against it, shoving it into the mirror. She had to grab the frame to steady herself. The surface of the mirror had turned black, glowing at the edges.

She could just walk through. Step into wherever the ghost had gone. The wind changed direction, pulling into the mirror, guiding her in.

Maybe she would find Duncan.

Maybe everything would be okay.

She closed her eyes and heaved the mirror over.

It landed on its front with a tremendous crash. Glass scattered around her feet. Something black and viscous oozed through the broken shards like molasses, pooling on the cement before disappearing.

The lights that hadn't shattered buzzed on. Overhead one of the windows had broken. Unfiltered sunlight streamed through in a brilliant gold shaft, catching motes of light. Shards of glass and bits of tree littered the bar as if an immense storm had ripped through the room. She could smell alcohol from where she was standing. Some of the bottles must have exploded.

She wanted to sit down, but there was broken glass everywhere.

"Holy crap." Max stepped next to her. "That thing…it nearly killed us. Are you okay?"

They took the arm that the ghost had grabbed. Her hoodie sleeve had ripped, but underneath her skin was whole, mottled blue and purple.

"Oh man I am… not a fan of this." Gideon sat up. "Oh, ghosts can hit really hard. Or was that a demonic entity? It felt demonic."

"Sometimes when people fall off of things, it was a ghost," Jo said, walking the rest of the way down the stairs. "Well. That was a mess."

"I broke the mirror," Shay said. Her voice sounded small.

"You did the right thing," Jo said. "There could have been nothing but endless space on the other side, we don't know. And I couldn't ward it. There just wasn't time. We'll figure out another way."

"Yeah," Shay tried to sound like she believed it.

"And figure out how to handle your seven years of bad luck," Max said, clearly trying to lighten the mood.

Shay wanted to fall into her misery and stay there for a while, but she attempted a smile instead. "I'll have to reflect on my actions."

"Boo," Max said, but there wasn't any heat in it.

"We should go," Gideon suggested.

"Not until we get a look at Shay's ankle." Max helped her over to one of the few stools that hadn't fallen.

They all jumped when Morgan slammed a hefty first aid kit onto the bar. Her expression was colder than the ghost. "Wrap it up, then get the hell out of my bar."

Chapter 15: Mildly Wrecked

Shay leaned back into Jo's couch. It nearly engulfed her.

Max drove back to the shop, only stopping to get some terrible but otherwise unmemorable food. Shay was glad to not be moving anymore, embraced by the comfort of an old grandma couch with her injured ankle propped up on a beaded footstool.

The particulars of the living room had escaped her the night before. In the light she could see it was decorated in a "tornado through an antique store" style. Nothing matched, not even the doilies haphazardly layered on every available surface like pastel snow.

"I should open the shop." Jo didn't move from the armchair she'd sunk herself into. She'd checked over Shay, used some ointment that unsurprisingly smelled like lavender on her arm, and sat down looking pale and exhausted.

"Can you teach me to do that candle thing?" Shay asked. "Looked useful."

"That would depend entirely on you," Jo said.

Shay pulled herself out of the couch to lean forward. "What do you mean?"

"Well, no offense, but you don't seem to be particularly open to the energies of the universe," Jo said. Shay couldn't help making a face and Jo pointed at her. "See? This is exactly what I mean."

"I could be open," Shay said. Jo's eyebrows rose. "I could be!"

"Magic isn't flashy, or exciting, and it's a lot of trusting yourself and your tools," Jo said.

Shay frowned. "But that's not what your magic looked like."

"What it looked like?" Jo frowned at her.

"You…you know." Shay made some completely indecipherable motions with her hands. "It was like bam bam, and you blocked it, and your candle was all woosh, and-"

Jo frowned. "I have no idea what you're talking about."

"The…the light," Shay said. "That it was hitting. Why are you staring at me like I'm a crazy person, it was your magic stopping the ghost, not mine."

"Because there's nothing to see," Jo said. "I honestly have no idea what you're talking about."

"Oh." Shay blinked. "It looked…maybe I hit my head."

Jo looked very concerned. "Did you hit your head?"

"I don't think so?" Shay admitted. "Maybe it was just everything going on."

"Maybe." Jo didn't seem very convinced.

They were interrupted by Max and Gideon bringing tea from the kitchen. Max handed Shay her mug before sitting down, their weight buoying her up from the couch depths. "Don't worry, there's barely any tea in there at all."

"Exactly how I like it." She wrapped her fingers around the ceramic, letting the heat sink into her hands. The ghost marks were the worst she had seen them, nearly black in places on her arms. Her ribs ached and her ankle still throbbed, though the bag of frozen peas was helping.

"Here you go." Gideon gave Jo another mug and she smiled gratefully. "You want me to open shop? I can watch it while I go through the video I took. Might not be much on there, but it's pretty mindless work. I can do both."

"That would be amazing, thank you so much." Jo stood up. "I'll show you how to run the register app."

Once they were gone Max picked up one of the doilies on the arm of the couch. "This is very comfortable, but these are weirding me out."

"Jo said the house was her grandma's, maybe they were hers," Shay said. "Or, y'know, she's kind of like a grandma already? Maybe she makes them."

"Or maybe they're wards against evil." Max put it back.

"A seal against the evil in this couch called sloth," Shay said.

"Sloth is a couch?"

"If lust is an attractive woman, then yes."

Max considered. "You know, that does make sense. How's your ankle?"

"Better." Shay wiggled her toes. Her ankle was wrapped up very neatly. "Mostly stiff now. Jo put stuff on the marks, said that it would help."

"Good." Max's voice went soft. "I'm sorry about the mirror."

She took a sip of her tea. "We didn't know where it went. If it even went anywhere. It was probably a trap."

She'd explained what had happened in the bathroom to Jo on the way home. Jo nodded tiredly and said she needed to think.

"But we're here, we're safe, and I smell like old ladies."

"That's the lavender and cedar." Jo stepped back into the room. "It does make it smell like mothballs, sorry, but it's going to draw the ghost out of you. Not your ghost. Or soul or what have you. This is a terrible explanation."

"No, I got it," Shay said.

Jo nodded and sat down heavily enough the chair groaned in protest, but the old wood held.

They were silent for a little while. The time was measured out by the soft ticking of a carriage clock on the mantel. Finally, Shay couldn't take it and broke the silence. "Well. We trashed a bar. Can take that off the old bucket list."

Jo sighed, loudly. "That was not on my bucket list. Besides, even if it was, we only mildly wrecked it. At worst. It wasn't trashed."

"Darn." Shay snapped the fingers on her good hand. Her left was still too stiff to move.

"So we mildly wrecked a bar, and Shay was almost taken by a ghost," Max said. "That was really not great."

"Yes, thank you for reminding me that I lost a client, and a friend, and wasted everyone's time," Jo snapped. She leaned against the arm of the chair, rubbing her temple. The beads on her glasses retainer clicked together. "I'm sorry. It's been a very bad week. It's not your fault."

Shay was sure it was at least a little bit her fault.

"You didn't waste our time, we learned things. And I've been thinking. If Duncan was taken for presumably having some sort of abilities, and Shay was almost taken, then Arlo probably was, too," Max said. "For being a witch, maybe? It sounds like he could have put a stop to this if he was here. The important thing is if we find whoever's doing this, then we'll find him. Probably."

"I had considered that," Jo admitted, fidgeting with her cardigan. "What we need to do is find the source."

"I guess next time Scribbles shows up you can just let him yank me through a mirror," Shay said.

"No we can't— scribbles?" Max looked at her.

"Right, you guys probably couldn't see him well," Shay said. "Its head looked kind of like steel wool, it had all of these wires. It was actually horrible I really don't want to ever see it again."

"I couldn't even see it's head," Jo said. "It looked like a headless pair of coveralls to me."

"Me, too," Max said.

"Lucky." Shay would have sunk farther into the couch for a good sulking posture, but she was pretty sure the couch would actually come to life and eat her. Max patted her knee, so at least she had that.

"Wait, you saw something different with the first ghost, too," Jo said. "And we never got Gideon's explanation of what he saw…maybe you did see my magic."

"You can see magic?" Max asked.

Shay shrugged. "Apparently. Hey, since I'm not open to the energies of the universe or whatever, maybe you could teach Max witch stuff. You don't have to be born with it, right? They'd be good at it, I bet."

"I don't know…" Max looked embarrassed.

"It's not a bad idea," Jo said. "But right now I don't think we have the time."

"Right," Shay agreed. "I think whoever was talking to me in the mirror is the person behind this."

"Or a super self-aware ghost," Max said.

Jo shook her head. "I highly doubt that's the case. Ghosts are like…well, photographs, I guess, is the best way to put it. The remnants of what someone used to be, but it isn't them. Fully aware ghosts are extremely rare. More often they're impressions, or residuals, some darkness left behind that the soul either couldn't use or didn't need."

"That's deep," Shay said, after a moment.

"It's things Arlo and my grandma told me about." Jo flushed a bit. "It boils down to a person being behind this, because it would take a very rare ghost, and I just don't see what the endgame for any ghost would be. This someone must have an incredibly dangerous ability if they can send ghosts to do their bidding. I have no idea how or why they're putting the mirrors in these places, or where they're finding such powerful ghosts, but I doubt it's for anything good."

"So, other than me going out there and getting kidnapped, or ghostnapped, if you will, how do we find them?" Shay asked. "Because if they're a person we can do something about that. Right?"

"I have a few ideas," Jo said. "But they're going to take a while. You look exhausted."

"So do you," Shay countered.

"I didn't sleep well," Jo said. "But I'll be fine. You have ghost marks to recover from. You need rest."

"I can help," Max offered. "At least with the front, see if Gideon has picked up anything."

"Thank you, Max."

Shay didn't really remember finishing her tea or lying down, but when she opened her eyes again a thick afghan blanket covered her. She wasn't wearing her glasses. Everything was blurred into softness. The light coming through the windows had shifted, slanting in thick, honey gold stripes across the wooden floor and faded rug. Max was sitting in the armchair reading something on their phone, their glasses perched in their hair.

When Shay sat up and rubbed the side of her head Max nearly dropped their phone, hurrying to sit on the abandoned footstool. "Hey. You kind of crashed out there. Feeling better?"

"Well, I feel less like a beanbag tossed in an ice maker," Shay said. She moved her ankle experimentally and to her surprise the throbbing was barely there. "What time is it?"

"Almost three," Max said. "You look better. What do you need? Water? Food? More tea?"

"A new hoodie." Shay looked at her bandaged arm. The sleeve looked like she'd stuck it in a garbage disposal. "And the bathroom. Move."

"Of course, your highness." Max stood and stepped away with a bow.

"And like, fifteen percent less being a smart ass. At least."

Max laughed and she huffed. Her ankle took her weight well enough that there was minimal hobbling.

She splashed water on her face and looked in the mirror. The light fixtures looked like snowdrops. They were pretty, but the light they put out was dismal. She had dark bags under her eyes and her face was pale.

"I look like a raccoon," she told her reflection.

In response, the darkness around her eyes deepened, cheekbones jutting forward, and skin going ghastly until it was just a skull.

She sighed and tucked loose hair behind her ear. "How did you even get in the house? Did you follow me here? Well, surprise, you stupid skeletal weirdo, this isn't my house. A big bad witch lives here and she's going to end your whole existence."

Mirror ghost clattered its jaw.

"I can't hear you. Are you spying on me? Or is this you without your little friend around?"

It shrugged bony shoulders.

"This is dumb," Shay said. "This is dumb and you're dumb. See ya, mirror ghost. Good luck with your non-life."

She dried off her face, flipped off the lights, and closed the door just for good measure.

"Where's Jo?" she asked.

"In the kitchen, trying to scry, but she says her most effective way doesn't work until nightfall," Max said. "She seemed really intent on doing something so I just kinda let her be."

"Think we could head by my place while we continue to let her be?" Shay asked. "I only packed the one hoodie. And it's Becky's dinner time. Kinda…missed breakfast, come to think of it."

Becky was technically Duncan's cat, but he always insisted she was both of theirs. Probably so Shay would clean out her litter box.

"Yeah, I think she'll be okay with it." Max grabbed their keys off the coffee table.

Jo was at the table, frowning at a spread of old-fashioned looking tarot cards. Candles burned on every available surface. At the other end of the table was a crystal ball, a metal pendulum, and a mirror. The mirror was cracked.

"Oh, hi." She looked up at them, her expression smoothing over. "You look better."

"Sure," Shay said. "What are you doing?"

"Trying every form of scrying I can." Jo sighed. "I'm good with cards, not so good with these. My real specialty is hydromancy. Since I can't use that until dark, I thought maybe some spreads would help."

She gestured to the cards. The Death card was right in the center.

"Yeah, seems right," Shay said.

"It just means change, though, right?" Max asked.

"Yes, but what is going to change… I don't know." Jo gathered all of the cards with a practiced motion and shuffled them. She fanned them out and held them to Shay. "Pick one."

Shay did, flipping it over.

Two people leapt from a tower being struck by lightning.

"Is that better or worse than Death?" Shay handed the card back.

"It's worse," Jo frowned at the illustration. "Probably a lot worse."

"…I could put it back and try again?" Shay suggested.

Jo sighed. "You know that's not how it works."

"Yeah, I know," Shay didn't want to look at it again. The people were simply drawn, but the silent screams on their faces made her uneasy. "Well, regardless of towers and death, I do want to go home and get some stuff. Take care of the cat. Would that be okay?"

"Might as well, while we're just waiting." Jo tapped the cards against the table top. "Bring me something of Duncan's, something that he values. It might help."

"You got it." Shay gave her finger guns and got an eye roll in return. "Speaking of skulls and horrible monstrosities, that ghost in the mirror? At the bar? It's uh…in your bathroom mirror now. So. That's weird. And I'm sorry."

"What?" Jo looked up at her, face absolutely disgusted. "Shay. How on earth did you get a ghost into a fully warded house?"

"You say that like I meant to do it." Shay did feel a little guilty, though. Maybe Jo sensed she couldn't use magic because she ruined everything. "Which I did not. It just showed up."

"I'll get rid of it." Jo stood up. "Not like I'm getting anything else done. Try to be back before dark, don't engage with any ghosts you see, and please bring back food. I don't care what it is."

"Can do." Max saluted her.

Gideon looked up from his laptop when they walked through the shop. "Oh good, I wanted to talk to you guys."

"About how cool we are?" Shay asked.

"Goes without saying." Gideon turned his laptop around and joined them on the other side of the counter. Someone was looking at books, but they didn't seem to be bothered. "Okay, so, I haven't had a chance to look through all of the footage. Here's what I got of when… y'know."

It was only a few seconds long, and so shaky that Shay could barely make out what was happening. Gideon paused it. "There."

She could see Duncan, a blue aura swirling around him, even though it was fuzzy and out of focus. "Yeah. That looks like the moment."

"Now, this looked familiar, so I went back through some of our older stuff." Gideon opened another file. The camera was completely stationary this time, showing a doorway at nighttime. Moonlight flooded in from above, the light bright enough that it was regular video. A little dark, but she could see the broken-down room around the doorway.

Taylor walked in, a flashlight in hand. She pointed it down before it could glare off of the camera. In her other hand she was holding a fancy looking recorder.

Her mouth moved, but there was no audio. She waited several moments before she spoke again, but seemed halfway through her sentence when an odd look crossed her face and she dropped the recorder. The moonlight seemed brighter, for a moment, then she leaned over, picked it up, and walked out of the room.

"That was weird," Shay said.

"Look." Gideon backed it up and paused the video. "Around her, see? Blue light."

"So…this has happened before?" Shay suggested. "Has she been acting…weird?"

"I don't know, she seemed normal." Gideon shrugged. "Maybe it was a temporary thing. A test run, possibly?"

"Or she could have brought the mirror in," Max said.

"Maybe." Gideon frowned at the video. "Like I said, she's been normal, when she comes in. Now, I couldn't find the audio file associated with this, but if I dig it up I'll let you know. I'll try to see if there's anything the camera picked up, too."

"Thanks," Shay said.

"If you hear anything give us a call," Max said. "See you in a bit."

They left the shop into the late afternoon sunshine. Shay closed her eyes and just let it warm her skin. A breeze tossed a few leaves down the road and made her shiver, climbing into Max's car.

A few minutes later they were walking up the stairs to the apartment.

She could hardly believe it had only been two days since she'd walked the same path. It felt like everything had changed. Jo picking the death card every time suddenly made terrifying sense.

She unlocked the door and expected a black blur to come flying out of nowhere, demanding food, pats, and that Shay never leave her alone ever again.

The apartment was silent, the front room empty.

She knew Duncan wouldn't be there, but some part of her still expected him on the couch, or in the kitchen. The dark quiet was crushing. For a moment it left her breathless.

"Where's Becky?" Max asked, and the feeling eased.

Shay kicked off her shoes. "I dunno. Sleeping under a bed, maybe. I just want to sit. For a second."

After the dumpster fire that was her college experience, she'd moved in with Duncan. It hadn't been for very long, really, just a few months, but it was home. There was an impermanence to apartment living, but this was where her stuff was, where she binged bad tv with her brother, and burned popcorn almost nine times out of ten. So, it was home.

She flopped down on the couch, propping her foot up on the coffee table.

"You doing okay?" Max sat down next to her, a little more mindful of gravity and cushion integrity.

"You have got to stop asking me that," Shay said. When they looked a little hurt, she sighed. "Sorry. I feel like everyone is just checking on me all the time and I keep saying I'm okay but…I'm not. Duncan's gone, and I gotta get him back. And find whoever took him. And punch the ghost out of them. It's just a lot, y'know?"

"Yeah, I know." Max looked at her. "Wait. Do you think they're possessed, too? Does that even make sense? Oh, wait, you were talking about murder."

"You're so good, Max." She patted their knee. "Never change. Are you okay?"

"What, me? Yeah, I'm totally good. Jo kept me safe when we were fighting that ghost, and I mean, yes, I probably lost about twenty years off my life span when you got lifted up in the air, but you're okay, I think, and I'm okay. And everything is okay."

"Yeah, I know, but how are you doing like…emotionally."

"Oh! Well, You know. Just. Trucking. Trucking along," Max said.

Which was probably code for so anxious that they could no longer feel it. "Keep on trucking, Max. Thanks. For, y'know, sticking around in all of this. I know it's a mess, and I'm a mess. There's just a lot of mess here."

"It's cool, I'm really good at cleaning," Max said.

"Aww you." Shay poked their shoulder. "I knew there was a reason I kept you around."

"Yeah, to clean your room."

They both laughed and lapsed into silence. It was more comfortable than the one at Jo's and she did feel a little better. Max was magical like that, with or without witch training.

She gave it another minute before she stood up and stretched. "Okay, I'm going to hunt down a decent jacket, you find Becky."

"Got it." Max stood, too.

Shay found Duncan's leather jacket hanging in the coat closet. He never actually wore it, for some reason that probably had everything to do with it not looking cool on him at all. It fit a little big on her, but it was workable. It even had a hood made of sweatshirt material, so it wasn't too different from her normal hoodie.

She even found a pair of her hiking boots in the closet. They probably had better traction than her chucks so she shoved them on and laced them up.

"There. Ghost ready." She looked down at herself.

"Um, Shay?" Max called from the kitchen. "I think we have a problem."

Chapter 16: Poltergeist

A thrill of cold shocked its way up Shay's spine.

The apartment felt normal to her. Stuffy, lonely, and a little cold. That was the day to day. If it felt weirdly empty, the reason was obvious.

She stood up, quietly, walking as quietly as she could into the kitchen while wearing boots. She kept her voice as calm as possible. "What is it?"

"There's a note on the fridge."

She blinked, her shoulders relaxing, stepping into the kitchen. "How is that a problem?"

"Well, look." Max gestured to the fridge.

Duncan had a magnetic whiteboard on the door that they'd initially agreed would be a chore chart, but it had actually just been used for doodles and insults for months.

The last few weeks of scribbling had been wiped clean to leave a single message.

I boarded the cat. I'm not a monster.

The handwriting was unmistakably Duncan's. The use of periods was not. The smiley face next to it might have been.

She realized Max was looking at her expectantly. "Okay. A body snatching ghost has possessed my brother, knows where he lives, and…boarded the cat."

She took a deep breath and released it slowly through her nose, even though all she wanted to do was start laughing hysterically.

"What do we do?" Max asked.

"We get out of here," Shay said. "If it knows where we are, so does its…I don't know. Friend thing. The person with the mirrors. Doesn't matter, we're leaving."

The thought of Scribbles, the Wire Ghost, or Jack Skellington in her house made her want to scream.

Max nodded, shouldering their bag and following Shay to the door. The apartment seemed darker. She hoped it was just paranoia.

She felt the cold radiating from the door handle before she touched it. She tugged her sleeve over her hand before she tried to turn it, but the iciness of it sunk in through the leather.

It didn't budge.

"We shouldn't have come here." Max's voice cracked. "What do we do? Shay? Shay what do we do?"

"We calm down," Shay said, ignoring how her voice was hoarse like she had screamed. "Okay uh. Duncan said he climbed up the trellis to the balcony, once, maybe we can climb down? No wait, he's a liar, there's no way that works."

Her stomach lurched even as she considered it. Just thinking of being on the balcony, looking down towards the parking lot, she didn't think she could even get over the railing.

They were on the third floor, if the trellis broke it could be a lot worse than a mildly injured ankle. The twisted fear of the faces on the tower card rose unbidden in her mind and she swallowed, hard.

"I'll text Jo." Max already had their phone out. "Maybe she can help."

"Good idea," Shay said. "I can't see anything, so I think we're safe for the moment."

Cold settled around her like a weight and something whispered so close to her ear she swore she felt it. *"Even you can't see everything."*

She swatted at the space next to her shoulder.

It laughed, the chill flowing away from her.

"Shay?"

"Do you have any of that wonder salt on you?" she kept her voice low, though she doubted it would help. The panic bubbling up her throat made her shake. "A sachet? A candle? Anything?"

"No?" Max sounded more scared than she felt.

She had to keep them safe. Nothing else mattered. "Okay. Well. We have company."

Something crashed in the kitchen. The tv fell over. It landed on the carpet with a thud. Max squeaked and stepped closer to her. Her downstairs neighbors banged on the ceiling.

"You should have gone through the mirror when you had the chance," the voice sounded like several people whispering at once. It deepened into a singular, inhuman growl. *"Don't worry, you won't get a choice this time."*

Shay hit the door with her shoulder, but it didn't even budge. Books flew from a shelf. Papers left on the coffee table fluttered like someone was passing them. She narrowed her eyes and thought she made out a shape, a shimmer in the air, but it was gone before she could really pin it down.

"Poltergeist," Max breathed.

She darted forward, lunging for a lighter and a scented candle. It was white, like Jo's had been. It had to help. Before she could use it the lighter was ripped from her hand. It hit the wall hard enough that the plastic casing shattered. Lighter fluid spilled on the carpet. The candle followed, glass cracking, leaving a hole in the sheetrock.

Max gently pushed her out of the way. They slammed into the door with their entire weight.

It didn't even rattle in the frame.

The lighter fluid caught on fire.

"Oh crap." She grabbed a ratty blanket off the back of the couch. She smothered the flames, stamping on the smoking blanket for good measure. The smoke alarm started blaring. "I know! I know!"

"Shay…" Max said.

She turned around. Orange light spilled from the kitchen. Smoke billowed up around the door. "Max! Get down!"

She ran into the kitchen without seeing if they listened to her. The stove top was on fire. Flames licked their way up the cabinets, catching on the old paint and spreading across the ceiling. Hot air and smoke hit her lungs. She started coughing.

She yanked open the cabinet beneath the sink. She saw the red body of the extinguisher, but the doors slammed before she could reach for it. She pulled, leaning back hard. Nothing happened.

Max ignored her and followed her into the room. They grabbed a dishtowel. It ripped in half in their hands.

"C'mon!" They grabbed her shoulders and yanked her out of the kitchen. Just in time. The jars above the stove exploded, one by one, scattering glass, oil, and a variety of spices into the fire, forcing the flames higher and hotter. Shay's face felt sunburnt.

"What do we do?" Max asked her, again. They were coughing, too, holding the half of the dish towel against their mouth.

"*The mirror.*"

"Nothing else left to do," Shay admitted. Max's hand was still around her and she used it to drag them down the hall.

Her throat was on fire, her lungs felt starved for air, and her eyes stung and watered. More things crashed and banged around the apartment, adding to the cacophony of the fire alarm. Books exploded into flurries of loose pages. The tv remote was stuck in the wall. The detritus of her and Duncan's life came pelting from their rooms, bouncing around the hallway. She stopped trying to duck and just held her arm over her face.

She got them into the bathroom and slammed the door.

The full-body mirror hung on the back shivered, but it had suffered much worse treatment. And that was just since she moved in.

It wasn't glowing.

"Hey!" She rapped her knuckles on the glass. Smoke rose in tendrils from the bottom of the door. The mirror rippled and shook with each impact on the other side of the door. The sound, the light, and the stink of smoke made the whole thing a hellish nightmare. "Mirror ghost! I don't know if Jo dealt with you, but I hope you followed me! You have about ten seconds to let us in or you won't be following me anywhere else!"

"Can it do that?" Max's voice was barely audible. Their grip on her hand was too tight and their palm was clammy. "What if it's not safe?"

"Here's not exactly a sanctuary," Shay said. She knocked on the mirror again. Or tried to. Her hand passed through the surface like it was liquid. Beyond it was freezing, but before she could pull back strong fingers circled her wrist and yanked her through.

She was plunged into icy, dark water. Everything was frozen except for a warm, steady pressure on her other hand. Light spilled from the mirror behind, ghastly green in the world beyond the mirror. It faded after a few feet.

She couldn't breathe.

She did her best not to struggle, going against every instinct that was screaming at her to fight for her life. Something was pulling her away from the light. For a moment, she thought it took the shape of a woman, but it lost its shape.

They passed other lights, cold and green, but too far away. She felt like her lungs would burst. She closed her eyes against the strangeness around her, trying not to take a breath, trying to not pull away, just for one moment longer.

Abruptly it was warm.

She took a deep, gasping breath that was almost knocked out of her when she hit the ground. Someone landed next to her and she was about to scream when she realized it was Max, still holding her hand.

They were lying on a dusty floor. There were shiny, scuffed spots where someone had walked across it. A brick wall loomed over them.

A mirror hung there. It was huge, bigger than Max, with an ornate frame of tarnished silver. The surface was so oxidized she could barely see her reflection when she sat up.

They were in a large, nearly empty room. Light spilled from windows above them, almost orange with the sunset. More windows lined the wall behind her, but they were covered with a steel door blooming with rust spots.

There was a counter taking up one side of the room. Stairs next to it led up to a loft on the second floor.

She knew where they were. A good portion of her formative years had been spent up there, doing homework. Or trying, anyway. She recognized the steaming mug held by some sort of corvid stenciled on the window. The Raven's Nest had closed right after her junior year. It spent her entire college career gathering dust and cobwebs.

"Is this…the old café?" Max asked, sitting up and rubbing their head.

"Yeah." She shivered. Her jacket was coated in frost, but it was already melting. She shook her head and ice fell from her hair. Her throat felt like she'd spent the day huffing campfire smoke. "You good?"

"Yeah." Max nodded. She scooted closer and they put an arm around her, still warm despite their own trip through the mirror. She could hear their heartbeat. It was too fast, but still reassuring. "Just held onto you the whole time. Guess your mirror ghost came through, huh?"

"Guess so." Shay took out her phone, maybe to call Jo, but the screen was black and dead. She tucked it back in her pocket.

They sat like that for a moment before Max broke the silence. "Why The Raven's Nest? And what's this doing here?"

"All good questions," a voice above them said.

Duncan was leaning against the railing.

"Hello, Shay." The cadences weren't as off as they'd been before, but it still wasn't quite right.

"Get out of my brother." Shay pointed threateningly at him.

Not Duncan laughed and leapt over the railing, landing like a cat on the empty counter with a puff of dust. Cobwebs draped over the edge fluttered like pennants. "What can you possibly do to make me? This is the best host body I could possibly have, even if your brother is… chatty."

"Duncan!" She got to her feet even though it felt like she'd been dropped in a bag of ice that was promptly hurled against the wall. "Duncan, you have to fight it-"

"Oh, please." The ghost sat down on the counter, putting ankle to knee. "That's not going to work."

"Any chance we can appeal to your better nature, then?" Max asked. They'd stood up behind her, putting a hand on her shoulder.

"Ha!" Not Duncan grinned at them. "You two are adorable. I'm so glad you made it through the mirror. There were doubts, you know."

"Are you the one who talked to me through the mirror?" Shay asked.

Not Duncan looked up from inspecting his nails. "Hm? Oh, no. That wasn't me."

"That would be me."

A young woman, maybe a few years older than Shay, walked out of the shadows of the loft and onto the steps.

Shay knew her. She had curly, dark brown hair that twisted over her shoulders. She was pale even against the cream of her oversized sweater. She was maybe a few inches taller, but everything about her was soft and unassuming. Even her voice.

Despite it all, she radiated cold, hard power.

"Taylor?" Max asked.

"Hello, Shay, Max." Taylor walked down the steps. There was something wrapped around her, the outline just visible. The shimmer in the air above something hot. She stopped at the bottom of the stairs. "I'm so glad you could join us."

Chapter 17: Finnias

Shay took a step towards Taylor.

A hot line of pain slashed across her chest, stopping her short. She looked down to see blood seeping through the teal of her shirt. The material wasn't touched.

"Clearly, you have no idea what you're dealing with." Taylor lifted her hand like she was petting something. Shay squinted and could just see the outline. The poltergeist was huge, coiled around her like a snake. The cold was intense. If Taylor was bothered by it, she didn't show it. "You all have some ability. Sight, touch, maybe even a little hearing. I'm almost impressed. Duncan here could be a decent medium and Max, if you tried, you could be quite the witch, couldn't you? Even if you were, I'd still be more powerful than all three of you put together."

"Do you want a gold star?" Shay was doing her best to not collapse into a gibbering mess on the floor. She was terrified, so scared it was making her lightheaded.

She stood her ground, anyway.

Taylor rolled her eyes, but the smile never left her face. "You get it, don't you? I can see it on your face. You know you've lost."

"You can't lose if you don't know what game you're playing," Max said. They sounded braver than she did. They couldn't see the hulking form twining around Taylor, visible in flashes and starts as it moved.

"Good point." Taylor's eyebrows rose. "I suppose I've earned a moment of monologuing. I can enhance a ghost's natural ability and using that energy I control them. But your little witch friend already figured that out, didn't she?"

"Mirror ghost," Shay whispered.

"It doesn't do you any good to ward your home if you don't ward all of the mirrors." She shrugged. "Anyway, you might be able to get physically violent with a ghost, Shay, but it makes you weak to them. I can make an army and there's not a thing you can do to stop me. You know I'm right."

"You super charged that poltergeist," Max said, realization dawning in their eyes.

"Indeed." Taylor's smile was too wide, too many teeth showing. "Mine, actually. Want to explain for the class?"

"A poltergeist is…I mean, sometimes they're ghosts, but usually they're phenomena of the manifesting ability of latent psychics," Max said, haltingly. "They usually disappear as the psychic gets older, or whatever caused stress for the psychic disappeared or…lots of reasons, I guess."

"Very good." Taylor sounded like she was going to give Max a gold star, herself. "Mine started when I was very young. I kept it. We've both become a lot stronger over the years."

"You have an imaginary murder friend, got it." Shay nodded. "Pretty sure I've seen this movie and it wasn't great."

"You're so much fun, Shay," Taylor said.

"And you're possessed," Shay said. "We saw the video. This isn't you, Taylor. You can fight it, too."

"Are you so sure about that?" Taylor asked. "Would you be able to tell if that was the case? It doesn't matter. Your part is done. Sorry. I'm leaving you here, and when the plan is finished… well. I don't think anyone in this crappy little town is going to survive. Even if you do," the timbre of her voice changed, going deeper, gaining in volume and power until dust was trickling from the ceiling, the windows humming in their frames, "there's nothing you can do to stop me."

Shay wanted to curl up in a ball and hide forever. "Whatever it is, I'm not going to let you do it."

"Oh, well, that's too bad." Taylor still sounded wrong. She cleared her throat, voice returning to normal. "Because you've already helped me. Sunset is soon and then I'd say it's going to be too late, but it already is."

"Are you a Scooby Doo villain?" Max asked. "Is this about real estate?"

Taylor threw back her head and laughed. "While I appreciate the flare of this old building, and all of the rest of this little corpse of a town, that's not what I'm interested in. I'm here for something much bigger than you could possibly imagine."

"Enlighten us," Max said.

"Would that I could, but sadly we simply don't have the time," Taylor said. "I'd get to the second floor if I were you, things are going to get interesting down here."

"Do you want me to watch them?" Not Duncan asked.

Taylor gave him an appraising look. "It's always like this with you, isn't it, Finnias? Fine, stay here. I don't need you, anyway. Come find me when it's over. We have a lot to accomplish."

He bowed his head to her. She patted his shoulder when she walked past him.

The back door opened, flooding the building with light.

It closed with a clang. The sound echoed through the empty building.

Shay let out a long, shaky breath.

"Your face is about to get interesting," Max muttered. "Sorry. She was scary. Let me see that cut."

"It's fine." Shay shrugged. It stung, but it was the least of her problems. "Just a scratch."

"We should go upstairs, as suggested," Finnias said. She couldn't even tell that he wasn't Duncan on the outside. His eyes were dark now, like they'd always been. If he didn't talk, she could pretend it was her brother, standing in front of her.

She'd found him, but he couldn't be farther away.

Her fingers curled into fists. She could touch ghosts, but Finnias was hidden, carefully protected inside of her brother. Could she punch Duncan hard enough to knock a ghost out of him? Could she have done that for Taylor?

"Just what are you planning to do?" Finnias grabbed her arm. It sounded layered, someone else's voice over his own.

"Nothing!" She tried to twist her arm away.

Finnias pulled her closer, leaning in to whisper to her. "I need you to hit your brother."

She could absolutely try.

He stepped back and she punched him, hard, putting everything she had behind it.

The look on his face was horrible, like it was someone else's, just for a moment. Dull green light wrapped around him.

It combusted, streaming into a fire that exploded from between his shoulder blades. Wind tore through the building, howling and roaring.

The flames swirled around them and flowed into the mirror. The sound cut off instantly and the dust whipped up by the wind floated through the air.

Duncan slumped forward and she fell to her knees trying to catch him, his forehead on her shoulder.

"Duncan?" she wasn't even sure if he was conscious, but she had to ask. She had to know. "Donuts, you in there?"

"Is he okay?" Max crawled over.

Duncan coughed. "Ugh. My mouth tastes haunted."

That was definitely him. He sat up and she hit him on the shoulder, gently. "You suck. I am so mad at you."

"Yeah?" Duncan ran a hand through his hair. The styling had not held up against being possessed for nearly twenty-four hours. "Aww ShayShay, were you worried about me?"

"Of course I was!" She was going to cry, and it was going to be ridiculous. "You idiot!"

"Is that my jacket?" He was blinking owlishly, like he'd just woken up, squinting at her.

"That's not important," she said. "Seriously, are you okay? You've been gone for a whole day. Like almost twenty-four hours now. I've been going absolutely insane."

"That long, huh?" He rubbed the side of his head. "Yeah. I'm okay. My eyes hate me. My everything hates me. But yeah. Okay. What's going on? Where's Finnias?"

"He…told me to get rid of him." She didn't know how else to explain it, or why he'd done it. The whole "I can touch ghosts actually" conversation could wait.

"Cool. Cool cool. Thanks for that. Now I need to get him back." Duncan staggered to his feet.

"What?" Shay's tone was surprisingly even, considering it felt like the bottom of her stomach had dropped out. She stood up, too. "No way, what are you- I just barely got you back. This has been the scariest twenty-four hours of my life. I'm not letting some evil ghost possess you. Again. Once was enough."

"I'm sorry, but he's not evil and we definitely need him." Duncan walked over to the mirror, putting a hand to the frame. "In here, right? He said that would probably happen. You can just yank him out, right? He said you could touch ghosts. And I'm like a spirit medium? Or something? Haunting it up with the O'Brannons."

"There's nothing in the mirror right now," Shay said. At least, nothing she saw, but she knew her sight wasn't perfect.

She hadn't noticed the poltergeist until it was too late. "We have to get out of here, find a pay phone. If those still exist. We know a witch, and she can stop whatever Taylor is planning. Or at least help find someone who can."

Not that Arlo was anywhere to be seen. Maybe he was wherever Taylor was heading.

"I think it's a little late for that to help," Duncan said.

"I dunno, Taylor seemed kinda…" Max gestured with one hand.

"Unstable?" Shay suggested.

"Confident?" Max shrugged. "We don't even know what all of this was for."

"She's going to rip the veil open and summon a…I don't know. It was unclear, honestly, but I think it was a demon," Duncan said.

"Ah, well, I guess we do know." Max looked like they really would have rather been kept in the dark. Shay could relate. She didn't know how to stop that, or even if she could. One super ghost was enough to take her down. Everyone kept throwing around the word demon, and she didn't want to meet one. "But why?"

Duncan shrugged. "I dunno, she doesn't exactly tell the grunts anything, does she? But Finnias knows. They're friends or something."

"Weird friends."

Duncan ignored her. "He can help stop her. So, we need him. That's why he had you punch him. It broke his connection with her. He's his own ghost now. Probably."

"Probably?" Shay's voice cracked.

"Good as I've got, kiddo, you gotta trust me," Duncan said.

"Fine." Shay limped over to the mirror. If Finnias could handle it, then she'd yank him out of the mirror a dozen times. She hurt, her ankle was throbbing again, and there was nothing more she wanted to do than just go home and hope for the best.

The best probably wasn't at home. She wasn't really in the mood to burn alive.

"Hey, mirror ghost." She drummed her fingers on the glass. Each tap echoed like a boom through the room, like there was a deep, cavernous space behind the mirror. "Can you get Finnias for me? I'll yank him out of your mirror. Duncan's body has a vacancy. I won't get you exorcised if you help."

"That's a horrible way to say that," Duncan told her. "Why—"

The mirror brightened and Shay stepped back. An insubstantial blue hand reached for her. A young man was visible in its surface, looking more solid and real than the arm already through, but still washed out and almost colorless. He was a little older than Shay was. His hair was slicked back and he was wearing a button-down vest and slacks that put him around the age of the mirror. There was a hole where his heart would have been.

"Well, guess we know how he died," she said.

"What are you talking about?" Duncan asked.

"…Nevermind," she said. She wondered how much easier her life would be if she just told Duncan the truth from the beginning.

Probably not even a fraction, because Duncan would have laughed at her and everything would have played out horribly regardless.

"Wait, you can see him?" Duncan's voice cracked.

"Yup." Max sounded proud, which was odd, but made her feel warm anyway. "She can see ghosts and you can get possessed, I guess."

"Wow, I sure won the whole 'ghosts are real' lottery, didn't I?" Duncan sighed.

Finnias reached his other hand through the mirror. Shay grabbed it. It was cold, the surface hard like he was still a part of the glass.

"Listen, I'm going to pull you through, but if you do anything fishy I will make sure you regret ever coming out," Shay said.

She yanked back, pulling him out of the mirror.

Chapter 18: Siphon

Gray swept from the mirror, turning the room dull. Max and Duncan stopped moving.

Color spread from where she held Finnias's hand, but it wasn't the colors the room had before. Red carpet spread beneath their feet and a thickly patterned wallpaper crawled up to form walls around them. Finnias was in color, too, his feet hitting the ground with a soft thud. He was pale, dark hair swept away from his face. His eyes were intensely gray. His waistcoat was charcoal and smooth over the hole in his chest, pinstriped with tiny silver threads. His hand was warm in hers. She could even feel his pulse.

They were standing on the landing of a set of dark wood stairs with the carpet inlay, patterned with little gold diamonds. A large, arched window looked out onto nothing.

Somewhere below she could hear the low murmur of voices, but the stairs themselves aborted in a gray mist only a few steps below where they were standing.

Someone walked up them, the mist swirling to form him. He was too blurry for her to make out and his voice too distorted to understand. He went to clap a hand on Finnias's shoulder.

Finnias yanked his hand away from hers and the scene disappeared, the old café achingly quiet in its wake.

"What was that?" Shay snapped, but if Finnias could hear her he gave no indication.

"What was what?" Max looked at the spot where Finnias was.

Outside of the staircase he seemed even more washed out and faded, just a wisp of what he had been. Duncan held out his hand and he disappeared.

Finnias blinked and rolled Duncan's shoulders like he was putting on a coat.

"That's better." He twisted at the waist from side to side. "It's always horrible to not have a body, and yet I always forget."

"You didn't answer my question," Shay said.

"Because I don't know." Finnias looked at her. Duncan's eyes were a dull gray, like they had been in whatever vision Finnias had unknowingly shown her. "It's never happened to me before, and since it clearly hasn't happened to you, we're both at a loss."

"What is happening? You know what? Since you're both being vague jerks, we're going to worry about it later," Max said. "What is Taylor planning? Why didn't you just help us before?"

"It was…" Shay sighed. "I don't know. I'll tell you later. You. Talk."

Finnias shrugged. "Gladly, but we should move away from the mirror. You never know who is listening."

"Upstairs it is," Shay said. Before they walked up she checked the back, anyway. It was locked tight, and she was pretty sure if the two of them couldn't move her flimsy apartment door against a poltergeist, they had no hope of getting through the heavy metal door.

They disturbed a thick layer of dust on the slat stairs.

The loft was empty and echoing. A wall of windows with a door and a balcony sat on the other side. All that was left were the umbrella stands, still bolted to the deck. Shay shuddered for a bit, walking to the middle of the room. She'd studied for a lot of tests in the corner, and now it was just all gone, like no one had ever agonized over their future there at all.

"An empty building is a little like a ghost, isn't it?" Finnias asked, watching her.

"I guess." Shay shrugged.

Max tried the door. "It's locked, but we can probably break it."

"First, I want to hear what he has to say," Shay said. "And if you know what happened to Arlo."

Outside the sun was setting, the clouds ablaze with pinks and orange. It did little to illuminate the empty loft. It was hard to see Finnias's expressions, and she didn't know them like she would have Duncan's.

"I'm afraid I'm unfamiliar with the name Arlo."

"Oh." Shay tried to not be disappointed. She had hoped too much that Arlo would come fix everything. It was seeming less likely by the moment.

"As for everything else, Taylor, or someone, at any rate, is a powerful spirit charmer. I needed to break the connection she had to me. As predicted, you did that quite nicely," Finnias said. "To really explain you have to know what a ghost is."

"It's people residue," Shay said. Max groaned. "What, that's what it is."

"She's right, though I would have worded it a little more tactfully," Finnias said. "I believe it would be easier to show you exactly what we're dealing with. Go look out the window and tell me exactly why going down to the street would be a bad idea."

"Fine, whatever." She apparently wasn't old enough to not sound like a sulky teenager. She walked over to the windows.

Whatever it took to move the explanation along so they could at least find a way to contact Jo. Shay had seen what she could do against a powerful ghost. She was sure she could do something, now. Anything.

Below them was a sea of deathly blue.

There were too many ghosts to make out the details. They crowded the street, filling it from one side to the other, as far as she could see.

The ghosts from that morning had been gathering there, not passing on like Jo had suspected. Taylor had planned for this the entire time.

"That's a lot of ghosts," Shay said. Finnias had joined her at the window, looking down. "But you guys could get help, couldn't you? I'm sure you could find a way to contact Jo, if you just-"

"Keep watching," Finnias said.

"Well, all right, I don't see how it could get worse, I… oh."

There was a ripple below them. Something brighter than any ghost moved through the rest like a shark, the blue parting before it. It was huge, twice the size of anything else down there, bloated and white. She couldn't look at it for long.

"Ghosts are memories," Finnias said. "That's why they're often tied to one place, doing the same thing over and over again. Sometimes, there is a spark of awareness, the need to manifest, to become something more solid and real. That's why you get cold spots and dead batteries. Unfortunately, when it's taken further a ghost can feed off of people and the memories of other ghosts."

"A demonic entity, right?" Max asked.

"Some call it that. I've heard it called a siphon. It becomes more powerful, but at the expense of everything it once was. We can't live again. We can't even get close."

There was some deep well of sadness, yawning beneath his words in a chasm. She couldn't look there, not for the moment.

"Taylor plans to rip the veil between worlds. It's not a physical place, there's no magic door with a world of ghosts beyond it. It's energy, what allows ghosts to manifest," Finnias said. "I don't know how she intends to make it work, but if any ghost can manifest, without paying the cost of energy it does, and she plants a spark in them…"

"They could all become siphons?" Shay had a sinking feeling she was right.

Finnias nodded. "And they'll be more powerful than any ghost you've ever seen."

"She's not summoning a demon, she's making demons," Max said. "That sounds…really bad. But if beyond the veil isn't a physical place, how did we travel between mirrors?"

"Well, mirrors have long been considered a way to trap spirits and…" a horrible look of realization crossed Finnias's face. "I…I see. Then that is her plan. The mirrors…oh. Oh no."

"You're going to have to back that train of thought to the station," Shay said.

"It's you," Finnias said. "She said you'd already played your part. I thought you were a wrench in her plans, or something else, so she trapped you. But no, she meant exactly what she said. She needed you."

"You're still not making any sense," Shay said. "I've only had abilities for two days, remember?"

"These abilities, as you call them, are hereditary, passed through families. One of your parents-"

"My mom is a professor of anthropology and dad teaches folklore," Shay said. She closed her eyes, taking a breath against a flare of anger and resentment she hadn't even known she was still carrying around flickering inside her ribcage. "My birth dad…well. I don't know. Where he is, what he's doing, but…"

"It must have been him," Finnias said.

"Shay…" Max put an arm around her shoulders. She leaned against them, glad for the support. "So that might be how she found out. And she-"

"Used one of her mirrors to start your powers, instead of waiting around to see if they developed on their own," Finnias said.

"We were sent to the house on purpose, and Taylor set it up so Duncan would be helping P.E.I.R.S.," Max said.

"And now Shay has ghost touch," Finnias finished the thought for them. "Ghost touch is just a way of giving physical form, even if it's temporary, even if you're the only one affected by it. Duncan was able to pass through the mirror because of me, but you created a physical space. And another, when you touched me. Any time you touch a ghost it will be worse. Taylor isn't going to rip the veil. She's going to tear a hole in the universe."

"Oh. That sounds. Really bad," Max said.

"So, we stop her." Shay felt like she had been punched in the stomach, but hadn't quite processed the pain of it yet.

"And now. We have to get out of here," Finnias said.

"Shay?" Max gave her a bit of a squeeze.

She nodded. She felt scattered, there was too much going on at once. She was angry, hurt, betrayed, and absolutely terrified.

She settled on anger. "Yeah. Let's go. She doesn't get to use me like that without it biting her in the ass."

"That's the spirit," Max said. They looked at Finnias.

"That was beautiful, Max, good job," Shay said. At least Max knew how to distract her. "But how do we get out of here?"

She looked out the window and froze. There were ghosts on the balcony, and more drifting up the stairs.

They were all looking at her.

"It's okay, the café is warded," Finnias said. "Taylor may not be a witch, but anyone with enough knowledge can ward a building. Ghosts are emotional beings, intent can go a long way," Finnias said. More ghosts were clambering up the stairs as the sun sank behind the horizon, glowing brighter than the dull orange of the streetlamps that stuttered and flickered like candle flames.

The first ghost passed through the wall.

"So much for wards." Shay backed away as it reached for her. It was an old man, with a neatly trimmed beard. He had spidery dark veins running from the black spots that were his eyes. Finnias swept an arm through him and he dissipated, but more spirits were coming through. "What do we do?"

"How many ghosts are out there?" Max stood in front of her. She doubted it would be effective, but she appreciated it all the same. "It just looked dark and blurry to me."

"Lots. Lots and lots."

"Scientific," Max said. "Wait! The tunnels!"

"The tunnels?" Finnias asked.

"There are a series of tunnels underneath downtown Teton Falls," Max explained, quickly. "No one knows what they're for, and all of the entrances to the outside are sealed, but they connect a bunch of businesses, and they're not all boarded up. If I remember right, they never sealed the one in the café basement."

"Max, you're a genius," Shay said.

"Well, they might be haunted-"

"Less haunted than the street," she reasoned. "Let's go."

They hurried down the steps. The floor was covered in a thin layer of fog and it was colder, but nothing had passed into the building yet that she could see. She tried to keep an eye out for the telltale shimmer of the poltergeist, but if it was there, it was invisible.

Finnias didn't even take the stairs, jumping down and landing like a cat. He hurried to the basement door, wrenching it open. The lock broke, pieces of metal skipped and clattered against the floor.

"How?" Shay asked.

"It's Duncan, well, mostly," Finnias explained. "Being possessed makes him faster, stronger-"

"More dramatic," Max muttered.

"Better hearing." Finnias gave them a tight, grim smile. "Down the stairs, now. Wedon't have time to waste."

Chapter 19: Tunnels

Shay descended into pure darkness and nearly lost her footing.

"Maybe you can see, wonder ghost, but we're running blind," she said.

"Wait!" Max hit her with their backpack when they swung it around and nearly sent her toppling. "Whoops, sorry, Shay. But I have something! Somethings!"

Something snapped behind her. Max tapped her shoulder and handed her the biggest glow stick she had ever seen.

"Were you going to a rave?" Shay asked.

"Shut up, it's a snaplight," Max said.

"We can discuss semantics later, get downstairs." Finnias closed the door, for all the good it would do.

The snaplight was about as strong as a candle, enough that she didn't fall down the stairs or run into anything.

The basement had sheets of cobwebs trailing from floor to ceiling. She avoided those, trying to ignore how many spiders she saw scuttling to the safety of the dark. Max was down next, Finnias bringing up the rear.

"Where is this tunnel entrance?" Finnias asked.

"Hold on, I'm thinking." Max swept the light back and forth. It caught on the webbing and they squeaked and shook it. Finnias rolled his eyes and took the light, yanking the cobweb off with no regard to spiders. He held it up himself.

The outline of a door was almost hidden under a layer of grime and dust. If it weren't for the two pallets covering it, Shay was certain they never would have found it.

"This must be it." He handed the snaplight back, yanking the pallets out of the way, revealing an equally grimy doorknob. He tried it, but it was firmly locked.

"We don't have a key-" Max started to say.

Finnias kicked the door, his heel hitting the spot right next to keyhole. With a splintering crash it slammed against the wall on the other side. "Yes, we do."

Fog trickled down the stairs.

"Max in front," Finnias said. "I'll bring up the rear."

Max nodded, squeezing past them to get into the tunnel.

Shay wasn't sure what she was expecting. Just dirt, maybe some stone, but the walls were a rough, red brick. Whether they had been set crudely or shifted over the years, it was hard to say. The ceiling, high enough it let Max walk without bending, sagged in places, more bricks billowing out under the pressure of whatever was above.

"This does not look safe." She held up her light. The cobwebs weren't as bad as they'd been in the basement, but glistening filaments coated the walls. "This looks the opposite of safe, Max."

"We can't go back," Max said. "C'mon."

"Why are these even here?"

"Honestly not sure. Opium trade, maybe?" Max said. "No one really knows, or at least I've never found an answer."

"Awesome," Shay said. "Drug tunnels."

"Quiet," Finnias said. "We don't know what's ahead."

"Wait," Max said.

Finnias let out a noise of frustration. "What now?"

Max took off their necklace, the little iron double horseshoe that was supposed to keep them safe from being possessed, according to Nana's shows.

"Here." They slipped it around Shay's neck, clasping it quickly. Their fingers were nearly as cold as a ghost's.

"But-" Shay looked down at the little pendant. "But this is yours."

"You don't say," Finnias muttered, and she seriously considered kicking him. Possessing Duncan wasn't going to keep him safe from her boots.

"I think you need it more than me." Max smiled. "That was all, I promise. Let's go."

Shay knew they didn't have time to argue. She tucked the pendant under her shirt. It was still warm.

They walked silently after that. The tunnel was narrow enough they had to go in single file. At some point someone must have had a party down there, somehow. There were broken beer bottles scattered across the floor, glittering pieces of amber that crunched under her boots.

She was suddenly very glad she hadn't enforced the "no shoes in the apartment" rule.

It was something out of a nightmare, walking down the tunnel. It felt as if they'd been down there forever, but in reality it had probably only been about twenty minutes before cold fingers grabbed her shoulder.

She shrieked and her back hit the opposite side of the tunnel. A dim hand reached through the wall, glowing so faintly she'd missed it.

"Go." Finnias pushed her and she stumbled, nearly falling. More hands reached through the walls and ceiling, one sprouted through the floor.

"I found the other entrance!" Max pushed at the door. "I don't know if we can get through."

Finnias pushed past her and kicked it in. Sheetrock and plaster rained white dust down on all of them. He kicked it again, knocking a sizeable enough hole that with a bit of lifting she was through and in another basement.

It was much cleaner than the last one and clearly still in use. The walls were shelves full of jars. Sacks of flour and sugar stacked neatly below them.

"Where are we?" Shay asked.

"I don't know," Max admitted, making enough room to get through from the tunnel. They'd left a sizeable wound in the sheetrock. "But the doors probably aren't locked and hopefully the place isn't swarmed with ghosts."

Hands were reaching around the doorframe, but their light was so weak she could barely see them. Maybe Taylor pulled all of the really strong ghosts that had been there up onto the main street to keep her occupied.

And to have an army at her disposal once the veil was torn.

She walked up the stairs, trying to ignore her ankle's protests. Once they called Jo she was sitting down and never moving again.

A place still in business had to have a phone. And an internet connection. Maybe even a way to charge their phones. If not, she would just look up Spellbound, let Jo know what was going on, and then keep out of her way for a while. She doubted she would be much use against ghosts that could murder her without too much trouble.

She opened the door. There was a kitchen on the other side, steel counters gleaming and empty. It wasn't that late, and any restaurant should have been open. She felt cold prickling up her spine.

Fog coated the floor.

The door slammed shut behind her before Max could follow her.

She yanked at the door handle, uselessly. She could hear Max and Finnias on the other side, pounding on the wood, for what good it did. The door didn't budge.

Something passed behind her.

She whirled around, but the kitchen was just as empty as before. She pressed her back against the door, trying to keep her breathing even, white vapor pluming from between her lips. She shivered and zipped up her jacket. The metal was so cold it burned her fingers.

"Shay?" Max's voice came through, muffled. "Shay are you okay?"

"I'm fine," she said. "I don't think I'm alone."

She took a few steps into the kitchen. The fog was so thick it was more like trudging through a few inches of snow. Something clattered on the other side of the kitchen, but nothing seemed different to her. A bowl, left on the counter, slid towards her, inch by inch, scraping against the metal.

Knives on a magnetic strip rattled and strained.

"I have to get out of here," she said, keeping an eye on the knives. "I'll draw it away and you can get out."

She didn't know if that was true. All she could do was hope.

She walked through the kitchen, slowly, trying to see if it was the poltergeist or something worse. The utensils hummed and the plates on the shelf above vibrated.

She stepped into the dining area. It was a sea of tables and booths spread across an old wood floor. The ceiling was far above her, lights hanging down from exposed rafters that she could just barely make out. Her snaplight made a little pool of radiance around her, but did little to help her see. The fog was nearly up to her knees now, so cold she couldn't even feel how badly her ankle hurt.

Her breath was too fast and shallow.

The noise stopped, so suddenly the silence was a noise all on its own.

Mist streamed past her legs, pooling near the entrance. Chairs slid with the motion, tables straining against their own weight to join them.

It rose up in a column and condensed into a figure.

It was massive, easily twice as tall as her even hunched over, spines sprouting from its back nearly brushing the lights. It was vaguely humanoid, but the legs were fused together into a single, massive trunk that ended in a tail, flicking too far behind it. Spindly arms ended in massive claws. Its eyes were twin points of blue fire, etching lines like veins that stretched over the head and down the neck.

The rest of it was white, almost too bright to look at.

The siphon.

It opened his mouth. It was too wide, too round, and far, far too dark.

The scream was thin and high. A discordant cacophony of voices. Shay slapped her hands over her ears.

It lunged.

Shay turned and ran towards the back entrance, ignoring her ankle. She heard it crashing through the tables behind her. A chair passed her head so close it parted her hair. It shattered against the far wall.

She cringed to the side, instinctively. A table rolled where she had been.

More tables were flung aside and the siphon screamed again. Shay hit the door but it was locked, the handle rattling uselessly under her hand.

She quickly ducked beneath a table, crawling away. It didn't take long to reach the one that had rolled past her. She hid behind it, sitting still, covering her mouth and trying to breathe quietly. All she wanted to do was scream.

It went quiet again. Deathly, menacingly quiet.

Shay's heart pounded in her ears. She bit her lip and focused on the pain, trying to calm down.

A hiss of something dragging filled the room. Shay leaned as much as she dared against the table, willing herself to become smaller than she already was.

The sound drew closer. The table moved, just enough that it pressed against her shoulders. She stopped breathing completely, didn't dare to move. What if it just slid through the table? What would she do? What could she do?

The table moved again, wobbling against her shoulders, and an enormous, clawed hand curled around it. The tips clicked against the wood.

She tensed, trying to be ready to move without making a noise.

It didn't matter. The table was tossed aside like it weighed nothing. The siphon shrieked. She threw herself in the other direction, tripping over the long tail and landing hard on her hands and knees. She crawled as fast as she could under another table.

It was done playing hide and seek. It ripped the table away from her. She screamed and it batted her to the side. She couldn't catch herself and hit the floor, rolling until her back hit a chair. She curled around herself and tried to breathe, tried to be anything but hurting and terrified.

The siphon loomed over her and she jerked away. Claws barely missed her. Five perfectly straight lines sliced the floor. A surgeon with a scalpel couldn't have been neater. She got her feet under her and ran back to the front door. Her breath was rough and ragged in her throat.

Her ankle couldn't take it and she stumbled.

The siphon hit her from behind and she landed on the ground, hard. It flipped her onto her back, pinning her down with one massive hand. She struggled. The fingers were frozen steel cords. She'd never get out in time.

The horrible ruin of a face loomed above her. The fiery eyes and teeth jutting out from the wide mouth made it a haphazardly carved Jack O'Lantern. Veins pulsed as if there was still blood and oxygen to move.

It tapped gleaming claws close to her head. The touch to her cheek was almost tender. It stung and something hot and wet ran down the side of her face. She smelled the copper a moment later and almost gagged. Blood.

She was going to die there. She couldn't move. The ghost was too strong, too powerful, and it was leaning over her. Would she even be a ghost, just lying there and letting it kill her over and over? Or would she just be gone, taken by the siphon?

"Shay?"

It was Duncan.

No, Finnias.

The siphon's head jerked up and it screamed, its teeth jutting forward. It crawled over Shay. She flipped over to get on her hands and knees again.

Finnias and Max peered into the dining area.

"Shit." Finnias grabbed Max and yanked them back into the kitchen, the siphon close behind them.

Shay reached deep down and found the strength to stand up. To move forward. She wasn't letting anyone hurt her brother or Max. Not even if it killed her.

"Hey!" She screamed.

The siphon turned to stare at her, eyes wide and brilliant.

"Yeah, I'm still here!" She yelled, holding up her hands. "I can touch you, right? Then I can punch you. Get your stupid ugly ass over here!"

It seemed to consider for a moment, torn between the two of them. It huffed, then charged at her. Its hands were up and its mouth was open so wide that it didn't have a face at all.

She screamed and punched it. Put everything she had into one swing, all of her strength and fear, knowing it wouldn't do anything but maybe slow down her death by seconds.

The ghost never touched her.

Her fist drilled a hole straight through it. With an explosion of displaced air it split in two. The halves held for a moment, flickering, then burst into blue flame, as bright as its eyes. The fire spread across the fog like it was oil.

It was gone, snuffed like it never existed. The temperature rocketed up so fast she was almost too warm.

She wanted to sit down. She wanted to scream.

Instead, she limped to the kitchen. Plates had fallen and shattered on the floor. A few of the knives were imbedded in the wall. Finnias and Max were crouched behind the far counter. Max had the metal bowl on their head.

"You really think that would have helped?" she asked.

"Shay!" They tossed the bowl to the side. It clanged on the tile but they didn't even seem to notice, hurrying to her side and hugging her so hard they picked her up. She normally didn't mind, but the pressure on her ribs made her cry out. They set her back down, gently. "Sorry! I just…Oh my god you're bleeding! So much!"

She lifted a hand to touch her cheek but Max grabbed it before she could. "Don't do that. You're filthy. There should be a first aid kit, let me get it."

"What did you do?" Finnias looked into the dining area, then back to her, quizzically. He really looked like Duncan for the first time, even with dirt on his face and white dust in his hair.

"I'm the baddest bitch in town," she said, sitting down without really having any input as to where. She ended up on the floor and found she didn't care. "I punched it out of the afterlife."

"Ah."

"Did you know I could do that?" Shay asked.

He shrugged. "I had my suspicions."

"Really?" She was too tired for it to have any bite. "And you were going to tell me this, when, exactly?"

"As I said, it was merely a thought. And it won't work with every ghost." Finnias folded his arms. "You disrupted its energies. Essentially, sent it back where it came from. It'll take a very long time for it to become powerful again, but it's still out there."

She nodded, not really sure she'd understood all of it. "So, I can make ghosts go boom."

Finnias sighed. "You can throw the energies that allow them to manifest into disarray."

"Pretty sure that's what I said. Please let me have this."

Finnias rolled his eyes. "Yes. You made the ghost go boom."

"Thank you."

Max kneeled next to her with a first aid kit. "That's my girl. Blowing ghosts up."

Max's approval did a lot more for her than Finnias's ever could. "Heck yeah."

"Okay, Ghost Fists, Vigilante for Justice, let's take a look at that cut."

Chapter 20:
Winging It (Poorly)

Shay sat very still while Max taped gauze to her cheek and wrapped her ankle back up. Their work wasn't quite as neat as Jo's, but they were significantly gentler. Probably because they were usually tending booboos for very young kids.

"Thanks, Dr. Max." She rotated her ankle. It still hurt, but she would be able to walk without help. Probably.

"You're welcome." Max started packing up the kit.

"We don't have time for that." Finnias was apparently finished skulking around. "We need to go, help me with the door."

"What, you're not going to just kick a hole in the wall?" Shay accepted Max's hand up. She didn't protest when they pulled her into a hug again, this one less bone crushing. It was warm and for the briefest moment she felt safe.

Finnias cleared his throat and Max stepped back. "Sorry. It was scary. Let's uh, let's go check on that door."

The door had an electronic lock. Shay hit the button that had an open padlock printed on it. The bolt clicked when it slid out of place.

"Needed help, huh?" She looked at him.

"All of my knowledge of any technology comes from your brother, so you should be shaming him." Finnias folded his arms.

"So that's why you're not having culture shock, you're stewing in Duncan's brain juices."

Finnias sighed. "I'm pretty sure you could be a little more eloquent about it if you really applied yourself, but yes."

"We don't have time for that, Finn, we have to stop Taylor," Shay said. There wasn't time to call Jo, either, and no computer for her to contact Jo with. It was up to her. That was more terrifying than anything else. She opened the door. "We'd better go before the police get called or something. That was a pretty big hullabaloo."

"A ruckus," Max agreed.

"Yes, I gathered," Finnias said.

"You have to use your own word," Shay said.

"A racket," Finnias obliged her.

"Very close to ruckus, but I'll allow it."

There weren't as many ghosts on the street, but there were enough that Shay was starting to think she knew what it felt like to be in a zombie movie.

"Where do we go?" Max asked.

"I…" Finnias faltered. "I don't know. Taylor kept much of her plan from me. I was only ever a pawn she had tenuous control over."

"So, you were a big old butthead all on your own, got it," Shay said. "It's fine. We'll wing it. We're certified wing persons."

"This way, I suppose." Finnias indicated down the street. "I don't have any other ideas, but we can't stay here. Don't touch any of the ghosts, Shay. Don't even look at them."

She nodded. They walked down the sidewalk, carefully. Max was on one side, holding her hand tightly. Finnias was on the other. Thankfully he didn't try to hold her hand, just stayed close, looking straight ahead.

"Hey, Finn?"

He glared at Max. "Don't call me that."

"Right, yeah, it's just that I can see the ghosts," Max said. "That's probably bad, right?"

A young woman roughly Shay's age in flannel and ripped jeans passed so close that Shay could feel the cold radiating from her. She had a silver crack spreading from the right side of her face all across her body, like someone had put her back together. She walked right through Max, who shuddered.

Finnias grabbed her wrist and yanked her over. "Geez, if you wanted to hold my hand you shouldn't have possessed my brother."

"Don't look at them," he said, voice low.

"Kinda not much else to look at here," she whispered back.

"Just stare straight ahead, you can't be noticed."

"I'll try."

She wasn't sure how she could stare straight ahead and avoid the ghosts. There were more the farther they walked. The whole street was awash with blue and green, the cold seeping through her jacket and air pressing in on her ears. The pressure was nearly overwhelming.

The ghosts seemed to be waiting for something. The anticipation curled in her own gut.

"This isn't working," Finnias said when they reached the street corner after what felt like a thousand years. "Max, watch her. Duncan has been briefed. I'll be back."

"Wait, what?" Max asked.

Light streamed from Duncan, forming the young man Shay had seen before. He looked more substantial. She could clearly see the hole where his heart should have been. He looked at her with pale eyes before disappearing.

Duncan tipped forward, catching himself on the lamppost. "Ugh. I've decided I hate that. 'Hey, I'm popping out for a bit, please try to make yourself useful'. Christ."

"Good to see you too, Donuts." Shay linked arms with him and stood a little too close. Their conversation before had been too brief, and Finnias was so different, it was hard to believe she had him back.

"Yeah, been here the whole time, but good to be driving again." Duncan patted her head. "He figured he could move faster if he wasn't 'bound by my useless flesh' or something. Also, he didn't appreciate 'a cacophony' so I need to find a better ghost friend. Sorry, ShayShay. It's been…a bit of a time. You all right?"

"Cacophony is better. I dunno. Right now I'm focusing on not looking at anything."

A car drove past. It was so inexplicably normal that Shay stared at them. She wondered what the street looked like to them. They certainly weren't slowing down for ghosts. Or for three weirdos hanging out under a streetlamp in front of an appliance store that had closed years before.

"Yeah, he mentioned that," Duncan said. "Ugh. Feels awful here. Everything is wrong, it's all misplaced. Not a fan. How about you, Max? Holding up?"

"Trucking," Max said, stepping a little closer to her. "I love standing in a crowded street when I can barely see the crowd. It's my favorite."

Duncan let out a strained laugh.

Shay was trying so hard to not look at the ghosts that she didn't see one pass straight through Max. Didn't even notice it until it bumped into her. She stepped back, but not nearly fast enough. A hand shot out and clamped on her shoulder.

Color bled into the ghost. He'd been tall and tan, with lanky brown hair and the scruffy beginnings of a beard. He was wearing a red flannel jacket and jeans that had seen better days.

The scene spread. Ice unfurled in the gutter, lights stringing themselves above them and up around the lamp post, cheery and bright reflecting on the wet sidewalk. It was snowing. The flakes disappeared before they touched her, but they collected on the man's jacket.

"How…?" he asked, looking at her. Even though he was right next to her, he sounded very far away.

Bright headlights appeared out of nowhere, the squeal of tires and bad brakes shattering the moment. A car barreled towards them. She screamed and the ghost let go, reeling away. The car turned into a haze that passed harmlessly around her.

"Shay?" Max had a hold of her hand, still. She hadn't realized that the warmth was gone until it came rushing back. "Oh man, what just happened? It got all foggy and you were here but not here…?"

"A ghost touched me," she said, trying to catch her breath. "It just scared me. I'm okay."

"Uh, we might be in for a mildly less okay time," Duncan said.

Hundreds of glassy eyes were staring at her.

"Oh crap," she whispered.

"Let's go." Max made the decision for all of them. "Finnias can find us. Or not. I don't care."

Ghosts closed in on them. Max pulled her around the corner and down a side street.

The dead were everywhere. Awareness seemed to spread and they all turned towards them, plants towards the sun. Duncan brought up the rear, swearing and slashing with the snaplight he'd kept a hold of. It didn't seem to do any good. She decided to not tell him that, focusing on keeping them from running into anything.

The sidewalk was crowded, and they were gathering in close. A large man grabbed for her arm and she barely pulled away in time, only for a tiny, old woman to step in front of her.

She veered at the last second, but it put too much on her bad ankle and she fell into Max. They kept her from face planting on the sidewalk, but just barely.

"There's too many," she admitted. "Maybe we can get into one of the shops, or up somewhere?"

"Nowhere's open." Duncan was looking around. "C'mon, Finn, get back here, we need you."

Max tried the door of the shop behind them, but it was locked. "We could break the window…?"

"Aw man, I can see them now, too. Why are there so many?" Duncan backed up to the window. "And that's plan B, Maxaroni and Cheese."

"What's plan A?" Shay asked, a little shrilly.

"Yeah, okay, good point." Duncan pulled the Swiss Army Knife she'd given to him a few years ago out of his pocket. "Give me like, five minutes."

"You have five seconds," Shay told him.

"Pressure, pressure." Duncan got to work on the lock. There was a snap and he opened the door. "Easier when you're not trying to make it look like no one broke in."

"Yes, yes, you have mad lock picking skills, we both know you got them from YouTube." Shay pushed past him. They closed the door and the pressure eased up, a little. It was a thrift store, which explained the lax security. Most shops downtown had metal sheets that rattled down at closing time.

"There should be a back entrance," Max said. "C'mon."

Ghosts were already passing through the front. Shay let herself be pulled through the store, holding so tightly onto Max's hand she was probably hurting them, but they didn't complain. They walked down aisles with hundreds of old things that should have held some attachment, but nothing stirred. All of the ghosts were behind them.

They reached the back of the store and Max pushed open the door, heedless of alarms. It swung easily in front of them.

They were in a dark, sloping drive circled by a chain link fence. Duncan scaled it easily, dropping to the other side and holding up the bottom. "C'mon, Shay, under."

"I could go over," she said.

"I definitely believe in your mad squirrel skills, but with that ankle you aren't," he said.

She scooted under, barely. Max had to go over, too. They were in an alleyway now, paved and incredibly dark. She could see blue glowing on either end, they were trapped.

"No way out," she told them. Ghosts behind them and all around. "What do we do now?"

The first ghost reached the back of the store, passing easily through the closed door and moving for the fence. It would be on them in seconds. Max and Duncan looked at her like they expected her to know what to do.

A car turned into the alley. For a moment she was back in the ghost's memory, the lights bearing down on her, but it stopped long before it reached them. The doors opened and Jo stepped out of the passenger's side, lobbing something over to them.

A sachet, bigger than the ones she'd seen before, landed on the ground next to her. It fell open and salt spilled from it, drawing lines on the ground, forming a complex circle around them. Jo and Gideon stepped into it just as it closed. The pressure in her ears disappeared.

The ghost stopped just short of the circle.

"Gideon?" Duncan stared at him.

"Oh thank god, you're okay." Gideon grabbed his arm and looked him up and down. "You are okay, right?"

"Yes? I mean, yes, I am. What are you…?" Duncan looked at Jo. "Aaaand I don't know who you are. What's going on? How did? Salt? Is that salt?"

"How did you guys find us?" Max ignored Duncan.

Jo smiled tightly. "I told you, I'm good at divination and scrying. I couldn't find our friend, but I could find you. Hi, you must be Duncan. My name's Jo. We're here to save you."

Chapter 21: Whirlwind

The circle quickly became an island in a sea of blue smoke. Ghosts pressed in on every side, sparking green when they touched the sides.

The salt held.

Shay had no idea how long it would.

It took a few moments to explain everything as quickly as they both could. Duncan still looked lost and kept muttering, "so witches are real now, okay, sure, we hate physics and common sense now, this is fine" under his breath. Or at least what he thought was under his breath. He looked surprisingly good for someone who'd been possessed twice, even though Finnias wasn't exactly gentle on him. She wasn't sure how his ankles weren't murdering him.

Jo explained that she'd tried to call her and Max. When they didn't answer, she and Gideon packed up what they could, kicked the last few customers out of the store, and headed over to the apartment to find them. Jo got to work scrying for them when she saw the fire.

Shay was impressed, actually. Jo really was good at what she did.

"You lit my apartment on fire?" Duncan stared at her.

"Technically a poltergeist did?" Shay winced.

"All of my stuff was in there!" Duncan groaned and slid a hand down his face. Shay decided it wasn't the moment to remind him that her stuff was there, too. "Uuuugh ugh okay. Save the town or whatever, then worry about how renter's insurance actually works. Fantastic. Love this for me."

"What do we do when Finnias gets back?" Shay eyed the circle. "He won't be able to get through, either."

"It won't hold for much longer," Jo said. "And once it breaks there's no way I'll be able to hold all of this off. Even I can see them. Shay, what did you do?"

"Nothing!" Shay said. "Okay, maybe some things, but they weren't my fault. This is all Taylor, and her poltergeist, and a little Finnias but he was under her control at the time so I can't really actually blame him it just makes me feel better."

"Taylor Stevens?" Gideon looked like she'd punched him.

"She's possessed," Shay said, quickly. "She must have been possessed when you went to that house, and…and it's not her. It's not actually her. I don't know who's really behind this, but…"

"Oh." Gideon looked less like his world had tilted off of its axis. "It's just, she's my friend. I haven't noticed anything. How could I not notice?"

Duncan put a hand on his shoulder. "When Finnias possessed me he had access to all of my memories and knowledge. With a few days, I bet he could act like me. If he wanted to."

"Probably not, I don't think he's a good actor," Shay said, quietly.

"Yeah, okay, good point. What we really need to be worried about is whoever is controlling Taylor has a poltergeist that can slash people open." Duncan gestured to Shay. Her jacket was still zipped up, but there was enough gauze on her face that Gideon was probably drawing his own conclusions.

Gideon huffed a breath. "I still don't—"

"Since she's possessed I should be able to help, but I think that's a later step in our plan." Jo eyed the salt line. "I think we should really focus on the problem at hand."

"Yeah, okay." His shoulders dropped. He looked crushed and Shay wished she hadn't told him who it was, for a moment. "Yeah. We need a plan. Um. Anyone have one?"

"I guess we wait for Finn, break the circle, run like hell?" Shay suggested.

Duncan sighed and pulled a hand through his hair. He looked pale and she hoped it was the light. "No, that is a terrible plan. Possibly the worst ever. How many terrible plans have you been making in my sort of absence?"

"Well, we trashed a bar," Shay said.

"And walked through a bunch of tunnels," Max added. They still had dust in their hair and a cobweb clung to their shoulder. She doubted she looked much better.

"Yeah, I remember that. Ugh." Duncan rubbed the side of his head. "Okay. Someone has to have a better plan than that. Also, seriously, is that my jacket?"

"It's mine now," Shay adjusted it. "Looks better on me, anyway."

It didn't, it was too big, but she was not giving it back.

"Yeah, okay, fine, I concede the jacket."

"Is anyone else seeing fog?" Gideon asked. "That's the ghosts, isn't it?"

"Yes." Jo looked exhausted and quite a bit older than her thirties. "Are you're sure you didn't see Arlo? He might have been possessed or tied up or…"

"No," Shay said. "We went all over that building."

Jo closed her eyes and nodded. When she opened them, she looked a lot more determined. "Then we do this ourselves. First, we need to find Taylor and neutralize her before she can do anything. Hopefully Finnias knows where she is. I-"

A light bulb down the street blazed to life and exploded, showering orange sparks onto the sidewalk.

The next one burst, and the next. Each light fizzed and popped in quick succession.

"You could get on that saving thing now," Duncan said.

"Wow, the gratitude," Gideon said, but he sounded scared, too. "How did I even end up here, again?"

"You promised you'd help," Shay said.

"Ah, right, my need to be a hero. Got it."

Max took Shay's hand. She squeezed theirs, hoping it helped.

"Get ready, something's coming," Jo said.

The circle didn't move, but the ghosts did. They made a path, and for a moment Shay expected a siphon to come barreling down it towards them. She didn't think a little salt would stop it and she wasn't sure that she could, either.

It was Finnias. He walked down the alley like he didn't have a care in the world and stopped at the edge of the circle, looking right at her.

"Is he here?" Duncan asked.

"He's here." She nodded. He nodded back.

"Are we really going to trust this guy?" Gideon asked.

"Does anyone have any better ideas?" Jo looked around their group. No one offered anything. "No? Okay. Shay's horrible plan it is."

"Hey."

Jo ignored her. "I hope he's fast. In three, two-"

On one she spread her hands apart and the salt blew a path right in front of Finnias. Icy, draining cold poured into the circle. Fog rushed in through the broken lines. Duncan shuddered and straightened.

He didn't say anything, just grabbed Shay's less tortured wrist and started running, dragging her out of the remains of the circle.

She'd thought it was cold, but once they were out of the circle it was freezing. Ghosts closed in on all sides, taking away her breath. They brushed against her, little bursts of their life bleeding into the world before Finnias pulled her away.

If anyone else was following them she couldn't see, too focused on trying to not fall even though she was numb and tired. It was an eternity of being dragged through a city of the dead, leaving bubbles of different times and places in their wake like a string of macabre pearls.

"I know where she is," Finnias said. She could barely hear him. "I know what she's doing. We have to hurry, she-"

A deep thrum rippled through the air. Shay felt it down in her bones. Finnias stumbled and stopped.

The other ghosts turned towards it in unison, like they'd been rehearsing for that precise moment.

"What was that?" Max asked. Somehow, they were right behind her. She shouldn't have been surprised, that's where they always were.

"Oh no." Finnias stared down the street. Even with the ghosts all around them she knew where they were.

Downtown was an eclectic mix of family-owned shops and restaurants, or it had been before most of them closed.

There was one house – The Governor's House, an old mansion made of dark stone that had been the home of the very first governor of Teton Falls, back when it was all farmland and a few homesteads. It had been converted into a library and gathering place of the Teton Falls Historical Society. At night, with the lights out, it was a dark monstrosity perched atop a perfectly manicured lawn. There were no ghosts that she could see through the wrought iron gate in the middle of the large, stone fence that surrounded it.

The noise rattled in her ribcage. She'd heard it before, on a much smaller scale. Back in the bar, right before they were attacked.

"Finn-"

Every window glowed.

Blue light poured from the chimney like it was water. The curtains flew back, letting more light spill through. It gathered around the house like a bubble.

It was so intense she could hardly look at it. The brightness gathered at the top and shot into the sky like a beacon. It ripped through the clouds and into the darkness beyond.

Wind yanked her braid over her shoulder. It howled and roared, pulling her toward the house. Her boots scraped against the sidewalk. Trails of spectral light streamed from the ghosts. They disappeared, one by one, into the light.

Finnias looked at her, wide eyed. "Shay?"

He was ripped from Duncan. Shay didn't think. She leapt forward and grabbed his wrist, leaning back as hard as she could. He was cold, his skin was hard, and her hands hurt.

She held on anyway.

And nearly fell over when the wind stopped.

They were standing on the landing again. This time sunlight streamed through the windowpanes. Dust motes froze in the beam.

Finnias was there, as solid and real as she was. His skin was warm under her fingers. The pulse in his wrist was rabbit quick.

"So this…" He looked around. "This was my life."

His voice sounded strange. She'd almost expected him to sound like Duncan.

"Don't you remember it?" Shay asked.

"No." That word held a lot of weight. "Shay, you need to let go."

"Not yet. I'm going to need you against that ghost vortex," she said. "Besides, we're learning so much about each other."

"Shay-"

"You know so much, about me, about this whole ghost thing, about how to stop Taylor. I can't just let that go. You might actually have answers."

"I don't. Besides, what more do you need me to tell you? You blew up that ghost all on your own." Finnias was smiling, but his eyes were deeply sad. "You're going to be just fine."

"Like hell I am." If anything, she held onto him tighter. She knew she couldn't stay like that forever. Already, she felt like she was being stretched thin. A few more moments might make her snap.

"I think I've been dead for a long time," he said, slowly, carefully. "And this is just going to tear apart the veil. It's really okay. You can let go now. I promise everything will be fine. After all, it's you."

Reluctantly, she loosened her grip. He slipped his hand out of hers. The world came rushing back, dark, cold, and relentless, so fast it left her ears ringing. She dropped to her knees, heedless of the rough pavement.

The wind died away, leaving everything too quiet. The house wasn't glowing anymore, the beam of light had disappeared, leaving a tunnel through the clouds directly above the house. Moonlight spilled through it, gilding the shingles and windows.

The ghosts were gone.

The streetlamp next to her flickered, just enough that she could see. Downtown was suddenly, achingly empty. Duncan was sitting up and blinking. Finnias was standing behind him, blue and faded once more. The night had scooped a hole in his chest. A cold breeze sent dry leaves scattering down the sidewalk.

"Is it over?" Max whispered. At some point they'd wrapped an arm around her middle, keeping her solidly in place. She hadn't even felt it happen. "Where did the ghosts go? Are they gone?"

Finnias settled back into Duncan. "No. They're still here. Something happened. Can you feel it?"

"I can." Jo nodded. "Let's get inside."

No one else looked like they had been yanked around by the wind. She tossed her braid back over her shoulder.

The gates to the grounds were hanging open. They swung closed the moment everyone was through with a loud, long creak.

"Ominous," Shay said.

The ground lurched under her feet.

She thought, for a moment, it was her bad ankle giving up on her. But the ground moved again, enough that everyone stumbled.

"What was that?" Max squeaked.

"We have to go." Finnias turned and grabbed the gate. He let it go immediately, hissing in pain. "Stupid human limitations-"

Hands burst out of the grass, brighter than in the tunnels. One grabbed for Shay's ankle but Jo threw a spray of something. The hands cringed back and disappeared in a puff of flame.

"Oh my god." Max pulled an arm around her, tugging her back to the wall. "Oh my god I saw those. They were so clear!"

"I hate this." Gideon was wiping his hands on his jeans like he could clear away the hands. "I hate this so much."

Jo gave her a frightened look. "She opened the tear."

"To the house," Finnias said. "We have to close it, now, before-"

The lawn rippled.

It knocked Shay onto her butt and Max stumbled, landing next to her. Gideon staggered but didn't fall, Jo and Finnias stayed firmly on their feet.

Another thud, like an immense heartbeat. Car alarms blared to life down the street. A few seconds later they petered off in a series of squeals and squeaks.

All of the streetlights went out.

"Get ready," Finnias said, dragging her to her feet.

"For what?" Max asked.

Blue pillars rose from the grass in front of them, oddly rounded. Gideon barely had time to get out of the way. Jo stood her ground, throwing a sachet at one. It burned up.

Shay realized what it was.

A hand, so big that the fingers were taller than her. It came down right where they'd been standing, moments before. The ground shook.

A featureless head followed it. A skinny torso and another arm lifted it up until it was higher than the house. It was almost white, glowing fiercely. All of the warmth was sucked out of the air. Shay couldn't breathe for a moment, the cold slammed into the back of her throat and spread through her, freezing her in place.

"Oh," Max's whisper was barely audible. "For that."

Chapter 22:
Conglomerate

The ghost turned to Shay.

It was still half in the ground, but it was large enough it could smash her and the fence with little trouble at all. It opened some semblance of a mouth. She could see the sky through it.

The sound that came out of it was enough to press her down to her knees. Fear spiked through her ribs, threatening to overwhelm her.

Fog she hadn't noticed before was up to her shoulders. It took everything she had to stand up again. She only managed it because Max was there to help.

"Inside!" Finnias yelled. "We have to stop her! That will stop the ghost!"

Max nodded and grabbed her wrist, pulling her to the house. They didn't even get close before the ghost was batting at them. It moved slowly enough she could see that it was textured. Like fur or feathers or-

Or many, many ghosts.

All of the ghosts, combined into one.

Max pushed her out of the way. They were knocked into the grass and didn't move.

"Max!" She screamed. Finnias yelled and the enormous conglomerate of ghosts turned ponderously towards him. She crawled towards Max, heedless of any danger. "Max? C'mon, Max you have to be okay."

They sat up and she wanted to cry she was so relieved. Their face was pale and they rested heavily on one elbow. "I'm okay. I'm just…so tired."

The words were slurred, like talking was an effort.

Shay checked their temperature. They were cold. She felt like her heart was cold, too. Heavy in her chest. "It's going to be okay."

Jo kneeled next to them. "C'mon, Shay. Let's get them inside. We can't get hit by that thing."

"Right." Shay nodded. Between her and Jo they got Max up and moving towards the house.

It was like wading through molasses – cold, difficult, and infuriatingly slow. Gideon yelled on the other side of the ghost and it turned towards him. Shay just saw it out of the corner of her eye, trying to focus on the house in front of them.

If they could just get to the house, Jo could take care of whatever was possessing Taylor, close the tear, and the ghost would disappear. Shay just needed to get everyone inside.

The ghost swiped at them and Jo pulled all of them to the ground. Cold air rushed over Shay. A hundred hands reached from the ghost to try to touch her. She flattened herself into the mist spreading across the ground. The moment it was safe enough they were running, as well as they could, up to the door.

There were sirens in the distance, but they faded out long before they reached them.

Jo tugged and twisted on the doorknob. "It's locked! It won't budge!"

"What do we do?"

"I don't know." Jo looked at her. Her eyes were wide, her face pale and scared. "Shay! Watch out!"

The ghost's hand descended upon them. She yanked Max down the stairs and Jo leapt to the side, crushing a flowerbed covered in glittering frost. Max stumbled into Shay and she couldn't stop them from falling. She controlled it so it was at least a little slower. Hopefully.

Finnias yelled and the ghost turned away, distracted for a moment.

"Shay, you have to go," Max said. Their voice was barely audible over the howling of the wind and a thousand ghostly voices high, high above them.

"Not without you," she said, a surge of anger getting her back to her feet. "C'mon, Max."

"Shay, I can't," they looked up at her outstretched hand. "I'll be okay."

She shook her head, her braid falling over her shoulder.

She wasn't going to leave Max. Or Jo. Or anyone.

"Stay low," she told them.

"Shay?" Jo extracted herself from a tangle of wilted fall flowers. "Shay what are you…We'll figure it out. We'll stop her together."

"It's okay." Shay smiled at her. "I'm going to be just fine."

"Shay, no."

She'd spent all night thinking once they found Jo, she'd fix everything.

But this was something she had to do. The veil had been torn because of her. Maybe she had to be the one to fix it.

Finnias kept dodging back from swipes of the hands. The ghost had pulled itself farther out of the ground, its reach much further. Gideon was by the gate, trying to get it open. One hand swung too far and demolished part of the fence, sending debris spinning across the street, smashing into the building and shattering glass.

She was scared, more scared than she'd ever been before. But she was angry, too. She'd seen the ghosts. Maybe they were just memories, but memories were what made them the people they were.

And now they were all gone, lost in a giant mess of a siphon.

"Hey! Ugly!" She yelled.

It turned, moving like it was underwater. It towered over her, even craning her head back she could just see its face. Hollow eyes stared down at her.

Ghosts were memories. Memories and energy all tangled together into some hollow semblance of what a person used to be. An empty house.

A siphon wasn't even that.

The conglomerate was even less.

She wasn't letting it take anyone away from her, not even Finnias.

"Shay! What are you doing?" Finnias yelled at her. She ignored him.

It was big, a lot bigger than the siphon.

"The bigger they are," she muttered. She lifted her hands and was surprised to find they were glowing. Not glowing, flames. It was cold blue, the same brilliance as the eyes of the siphon. Her hands felt warm.

The conglomerate reached for her.

She stepped back on her good ankle. The hand rushed towards her, filling up her vision.

She punched it, throwing everything she had into it. So hard she felt something in her wrist pop.

At first, nothing happened. It stopped moving, frozen half crouched, its fingers curled around her. The fire around her went out.

The ghosts wrinkled and pulled against each other, breaking up the form, hundreds of mouths crying in horrible agony.

Flame erupted between them, green and blue and absolutely dazzling. By the time it reached the shoulder the arm was falling apart, huge pieces sloughing off and bursting when they hit the ground. The ghosts screamed and wailed in a discordant wave of sound.

A burst of displaced air knocked her onto her back. She lay there, watching bits of light falling around her like snow, disappearing before they hit the ground.

She sat up and it gathered on her shoulders. She brushed it off.

Finnias was staring at her.

"How did…"

"Really big siphon." She shrugged, like it wasn't a big deal. She was exhausted, so tired she wasn't sure she could stand.

"Shay-" Finnias started forward. His eyes widened. "Wait-"

His warning came too late. Strong hands grabbed her shoulders. She was hauled to her feet. She struggled, elbowing them in the gut.

"Oof." It was Max.

"What are you-" she started to say, but before she could turn around strong fingers snagged the back of her neck like she was a kitten, holding too tightly. She flailed back and an arm wrapped around her, pinning her arms to her sides.

"Max?" her voice cracked.

"Not home right now, sorry. But everything you do to them is going to hurt, anyway," they said.

It wasn't them.

The horseshoe pendant burned with cold at her collarbone.

"Max, please, you have to fight it-"

Not Max squeezed the back of her neck so hard she cried out involuntarily, the pressure rippled down her spine. She tried to move but all she did was make her already bad wrist throb. Dark spots floated across her vision and her knees stopped working. If whatever was controlling Max hadn't been holding her, she would have fallen to the ground.

They eased up the pressure a moment later. "Would it be too much to ask for you to be a good girl, my dear?"

The way they said girl made her skin crawl. The term of affection made her want to puke.

"Who are you?" she asked.

"Does it really matter?" they asked, the slightest hint of a drawl drawing out and softening their words. "You're caught, little ghost hunter. You're a lot stronger than I expected. Finnias must be a good teacher. Remarkable, considering his mental facilities were wiped clean. Grab him. She'll want him there, too."

Jo grabbed Finnias's wrists, pinning them behind his back. He didn't fight her. "I think you can let go. She's not going to try anything, and neither am I."

"Suppose you can't do anything, anyway." The grip on her neck vanished and Shay stepped away, rubbing where not Max's fingers had left warm impressions on her cold skin. She didn't want to turn around, but she had to.

Max had a grin very much unlike their own, their eyes hard and cruel. There was a slight glow in their pupils.

"Pretty sure I took care of the ghosts," Shay said.

"We were held back, just in case," they said. "You are a tiny thing, to be causing so many problems. This one is big and strong, hell of a job trying to possess them. Wouldn't have happened if you'd just taken care of that ghost right away."

"Please let them go." Shay was shaking, so hard her teeth clattered together. She didn't know what to do. "Please. I'll do whatever you want."

"Oh, now, I'd love to, but I take my orders from someone else." The drawl was becoming more noticeable. "And I'm hoping she'll let me add this one to my collection. Maybe the purple one, too."

"Collection?" Shay didn't want to know what that meant, but she knew she needed to.

"Already have the big one that ran around with this one." They indicated Jo with an incline of their head. They must have meant Arlo. Shay had a horrible feeling that he wasn't in the house, or anywhere nearby at all. "These two would do nicely. I'd take Finnias's ride, if I thought it was worth something without him."

"Do we know each other?" Finnias asked.

"Remarkable." A slow, horrible smile stretched across Max's face. "Well, I suppose there's no harm. I'm Archibald. You really don't remember, do you?"

"Should I?" Finnias asked.

Archibald laughed. It didn't sound like Max's laugh at all. "Might be for the best that you don't, darling. We can part as unlikely friends when all of this is over. Don't worry, despite your wayward tendencies she's still willing to help you out. Always had a soft spot for you. Can't imagine why. Well, are we ready to go?"

Shay was on the verge of crying, of screaming, of something. But all she could do was stand there, shaking.

At least Gideon wasn't there. She didn't know where he was.

All she could do was hope he was safe.

She closed her eyes, trying to keep her heart from jack hammering out of her chest. She was alone. Finnias was right, she couldn't try anything. There was nothing to try. The conglomerate had been too much. Maybe, if she knew more she could punch Archibald out of Max and burn him until he gave her answers.

But she was spent.

And she couldn't punch Max. Not with knowing how much it would hurt them.

The only person who could free her friends was whatever was possessing Taylor.

Shay would have to go to her.

"Okay. You got me." She lifted her hands, hoping that her trembling fingers weren't obvious. "Take me to your leader."

Chapter 23:
The Tear

The house radiated a cold of its own despite the chill still permeating the October night.

Shay stepped through the front door, Archibald right behind her. She could have been walking into a freezer. The air burned in her lungs and escaped in white clouds. She shivered, hugging her jacket as close as she could. None of her possessed friends seemed bothered by it.

For the first time she was really, truly alone.

She looked to Finnias. He stared straight ahead like she didn't exist. There would be no help from him this time.

It was all down to her.

If nothing else, maybe she could dredge up everything she had left and punch the ghost out of Taylor for taking Max. The world could burn or freeze, she didn't care, but she was going to save Max.

The entryway was dark, but the hallway beyond it glowed blue and green, a blacklight not very funhouse. Streams of fog cut across the walls, ceiling, and floor with little to no regard for physics. It was even colder there, her breath seizing in her throat and her lips cracking. The cut on her cheek stung through the gauze. She shoved her hands in her pockets, trying to keep her fingers from going numb.

She had no idea what use it would be.

"Don't you worry, we're almost there" Archibald said. If it weren't for her then Max and Jo would be safe in their homes, not following her to uncertainty, possessed by something horrible.

Taylor still would have ripped the world apart, somehow.

Arlo would still be missing.

It was a cold comfort.

They passed through halls turned alien and strange by the light. The final room they entered must have been a study, at one point. Books lined the walls, covered in whorls of frost. Archibald shoved her in.

"I brought her," he said.

Taylor ignored him. She was sitting on the enormous desk in the middle of the room. The poltergeist was draped over her shoulders like a thick, horrible boa. Shay could see the shifts in the air when it moved. Her attention was trained on something to the left.

Shay wasn't sure what she had expected from everyone talking about a tear in the veil, but she'd never pictured an actual rip in the air. Blue spilled from it like a wound. It shifted, a curtain tugged in a breeze she couldn't feel. Sometimes it was barely there, sometimes dark, and for just a moment it was unbearable to look at.

Shay turned away.

"Oh, you're here." Taylor didn't seem too happy to see Archibald. "How about you be a dear and go catch up with Finnias in the hallway?"

"You owe me," Archibald said.

Taylor clenched one hand into a fist and Archibald dropped to his knees. "I don't owe you anything. Get out."

"Hey!" Shay stepped between them. "I don't care what you do to this asshole, but you are not hurting Max."

Taylor's face went from something horribly twisted to smooth and perfectly pretty again. "Of course, I would never. Go."

"Of course." Archibald stood up and bowed out of the room, closing the door.

It was just the two of them.

"Well, now that unpleasantness is out of the way, I'm so glad you could make it." Taylor smiled at her. "I am absolutely astounded you took out that big ghost. That was one of my finest achievements. I spent weeks getting all of the ghosts for it and you just punched it away. Incredible. Of course, I can just make more. A lot more, now."

"What do you want with me now?" Shay asked. "You have your tear. I can't stop you now. Just let everyone go, Taylor. Or whatever your actual name is."

It wasn't exactly a heart wrenching speech, especially with her teeth chattering.

"I don't really care what you call me. Honestly, I just wanted you to see what we managed to accomplish together." She shrugged. "Don't worry, this is all going to be over soon. First, I have a little proposition. A job offer, if you will. I understand you've been having a little problem getting one of those."

"You want me to join you?" Shay asked. Just the thought left her feeling sick.

"Well, yes." Taylor shrugged. "I have a few problems I need help with. Something you could take care of. And maybe we could forget about all of this?"

Shay stared at her like she'd grown another head. She was talking like she was being completely reasonable. As if the literal tear in the universe just a few feet away from her was something she could just drop because she was bored of it. Shay didn't even need to think about it. "No."

"Not even a lie to bide for time? You are not as smart as I thought," Taylor said. "Unfortunate. Well, then, I'll let your friends go. I promise! Cross my heart and all of that. But first I have to take care of one teeny, tiny detail."

"Yeah?" Shay was pretty sure she knew exactly what it was.

"You." Taylor lifted one hand to the poltergeist. "Kill her."

Shay barely got out of the way. The poltergeist came down right where she had been standing. The floorboards shattered. The floor shook.

Shay lifted her hands, just in time. It slammed into her. She hit the shelf behind her. Books rained down around her, paused in midair, and flung towards her. She ran, hearing thuds just behind her like footsteps.

The door stayed closed. Taylor sat and watched.

She was tossed onto the floor. The poltergeist struck at her and she punched it. No flames appeared, but neon green sparks flew. Shay's arm shuddered all the way up to her shoulder. It reared back with a horrible noise.

For a moment she was somewhere else. Sun and branches formed a lace above her. Someone yelled a name she didn't understand.

She was back in the study.

The poltergeist disappeared.

Shay looked around wildly, but she didn't see the shimmer in the air.

A book flew off of a nearby shelf and hit her in the shoulder. More books joined the first. She held her arms up to protect her face, spines and pages jabbing into her jacket and her less protected legs. A book slapped her upside the head.

Something groaned and she looked up. The shelf behind her rocked back and forth on the bolts that kept it in the wall. With a horrible crunch it wrenched free and toppled forward.

Shay scrambled out of the way. It hit the floor with a tremendous crash. Books scattered like leaves in the wind. Shay backed up to the opposite wall. The shelf behind her moved. More books slid out of their spaces, piling around her feet.

"That's enough of that, darling," Taylor said, like she was admonishing a child. "You can't very well bring the whole house down on her head."

It slid out of the shelf, curled around her throat, and squeezed.

She couldn't breathe. All she could hear was the blood rushing through her temples, her heart beat deafening. She was vaguely aware that Taylor was talking, but she couldn't hear the words.

The siphon had been terrifying, but not like this. She couldn't see the poltergeist and she had no energy to fight it. She was done.

Someone was yelling. It wasn't Taylor. She was standing in a field. Wind tossed trees surrounded her, the light in the leaves swirling in a dizzying kaleidoscope.

The vision ended abruptly. She was on her knees and the poltergeist was gone. The first breath hit her lungs too fast. She coughed. Her throat hurt, her lungs stung, but she could breathe again and was definitely alive.

Somehow.

"Are you okay?" Finnias asked.

He had one hand around Taylor's throat. She wasn't sitting on the desk anymore, standing very still. The poltergeist shimmered in the air around them.

"That's right, you little ghoul, don't make a move," Finnias glared at it. "Shay?"

"I—I'm okay." She stood up. She was shaking, but she was on her feet. And she was going to punch Taylor so hard it wouldn't matter what kind of powers she had. "She's mine."

"I'd love to let you absolutely annihilate her, but unfortunately, she's not really here." Finnias looked at her. "Are you?"

"Aw, of course you figured it out." Taylor smiled.

"What?" Shay was pretty sure she'd missed something.

"Taylor here is just an unfortunate pawn, a shell, for the person really behind this," Finnias said.

Her smile didn't change. "He's right. I'm only at a fraction of my power in this weak little girl's body, but look what I managed to do! What we managed to do. Imagine if I was at full strength? I could call your little friends in here. I could have them bend over and snap their own spines."

"And I could break your neck," Finnias said, like he was suggesting a Sunday drive.

"Oh, Finnias, it took a century, but you have finally gotten interesting," she said. "Still no memory though, hm? What if I could tell you everything? Would you really give that up for this girl? You've seen what I can do. You know where the power here lies. It was fun, controlling you before, but I'd rather work with you. After all, you-"

Finnias squeezed. "And I've seen what she can do, so I'm not too concerned about you."

Taylor looked scared for the first time. Shay was afraid, too, but before she could say anything Finnias eased up and she took a breath. "What makes you think I won't just abandon this body?"

"If you were going to, then you would have already." Finnias's smile was grim.

"You of all people should know that I'm definitely willing to leave behind a trail of bodies." Her grin was too wide again.

"But you're terrified of the tear, aren't you? You'll be pulled right in, just like everything else."

"Fine. I suppose I'll cooperate, then." She sighed. "Time to come back to mommy, dearest. It's okay, I'm sure you'll see your new friends again, very soon."

The poltergeist knocked a few things off of the desk and disappeared.

"Finnias—" Shay started to say. "She…"

"She has nothing for me," Finnias said. "I'm dead. It doesn't matter how, or why. It won't bring me back, so it's useless, isn't it? The only thing she could offer me is her real identity, but I have a feeling that won't happen."

She started. "Wait! What about Arlo?"

"You'll never find him without me." Taylor looked very smug. "Archibald hid him very well."

"I saw something, when the poltergeist attacked me," Shay said. "A field, that was you, wasn't it?"

"What does it matter? Like Finnias said, we're dead." Taylor shrugged. "Or might as well be."

Shay stared at her. Jo had shot down that it was a self-aware ghost, and Shay had listened to her.

If she had been wrong…

"What does that mean?" Shay asked.

The floor shook. Shay grabbed the desk, barely staying on her feet. The tear was widening, the air whistling as it was pulled into it. The entire desk lurched.

"You're too late." Taylor shrugged. "Too bad, so sad."

"I have to close this," Shay said. "Or it's just going to get worse, isn't it."

She didn't know if she could do anything.

She had to try.

"Shay…"

"No!" Taylor lurched forward, but Finnias still had a hold on her. "Let me go!"

"I don't think so," Finnias said.

"Get everyone out," she said. "You said it, right? I'm going to be just fine."

"You're going to die and you deserve it," Taylor spat."

"Shut up," Finnias told her, then looked at Shay. "I said that under duress, I'll have you know. Being sucked into a vortex and ceasing to exist duress. Your brother is going to kill me."

"I mean, I think he'd have a hard time of it." She managed a smile.

He let out a short bark of a laugh. The desk lurched again. "Stay alive. Don't look in there. I mean it. I'll be right back."

"Thanks, Finn."

He nodded, like he understood everything she was thanking him for. He yanked Taylor, still telling Shay she was about to die, out of the room. Shay heard Max say her name. The door shut before they could say anything else.

"Okay, tear in the universe." She turned to face it. "It's just you and me."

The desk made a horrible noise, scraping across the floor.

She had to work fast. How did anyone patch up a hole in reality? She couldn't even sew. What had she been thinking?

She was thinking that she was really, really angry.

Angry that she'd been used in this plan, that somehow her dad figured into everything, that someone could just take over people's lives to get whatever they wanted. She stepped forward, the fire of her anger fueling her determination, looking carefully at the ground.

She grabbed the edge.

It was cold. Colder than anything she'd ever felt. Worse than the mirror. Pain jolted through her whole body. She barely bit back a scream. It came out as a whimper.

It was excruciating, and slow, but she felt it moving in her hands. The tear wanted to close. It didn't want to be a gaping hole in the air.

She glanced up when her fingers slipped.

It was only for an instant before she looked away again, but she saw stars. An infinite, sprawling universe far beyond the tiny rip. At the center was something so bright and beautiful that it made her heart hurt in a way nothing ever had. It ignited a longing that was terrible and all encompassing.

She could look again. She could step through, right now. There would be no more pain, no more terror. Just an end.

Frost scrawled across her glasses and a pale blue hand pressed itself over her eyes. She was on the landing again and the hand turned warm and solid. Finnias's voice was so close she could feel it. "I told you not to look."

Then he was gone. She was shaking, staring at the ground, trying to hold the universe together with just her hands.

"Come on. We have this."

She looked up, even though she knew she shouldn't.

Finnias was on the other side of the tear.

"Finn-"

"I'm going to help you." He looked immeasurably sad.

All she could see behind him was darkness. There was no light, not anymore. Something was there, even she could feel it. Something horrible and huge beyond comprehension.

"We have to close it. Now, Shay."

She didn't want to, but she nodded.

Together, they yanked the tear closed. She barely got her fingers out before it sealed up with a sound like a gunshot. She was tossed across the room like a rag doll. The desk crashed into the wall. The glowing faded.

She closed her eyes.

Chapter 29: Aftermath

"Shay!"

She wanted to tell Duncan to go away, but she couldn't seem to get her mouth to work. Her eyes were closed but that seemed out of her control, too. She was drifting and weightless.

Something stung on her cheek and she lashed out.

"Ow!"

She nearly bonked heads with Max.

"Oh, geez, Shay. You scared the crap out of me." Max pulled her into a hug that was clearly meant to be gentle, but she felt every new bruise protest. "You're freezing."

"More importantly, she did hit me," Duncan was glaring at her.

"Well, you slapped me. I think." The side of her face still smarted. It was a tiny hurt she could focus on. She'd never run a marathon, but she imagined it was how she would feel if she made an attempt. Providing marathons had a portion where the spectators threw giant chunks of ice at the participants.

"Oh, it was a little love tap," Duncan said. "You're fine, and you're awake."

"That you, Donuts?" she asked.

"The whole dozen. Give or take."

"What happened?" Jo asked. She was standing a little further back. "Did you see Arlo?"

She leaned away from Max to look at her hands. The only light in the study was a flashlight they'd stuck on the floor. She had no idea where it had come from, but it at least made it easy to see their faces.

And that her hands were normal. Bruised and scraped, but normal, not even a hint of a mark. She breathed out, slowly. "No. Archibald has him."

"Who?" Jo asked.

"The ghost that was…Where's Taylor? She'll know where he is."

"Out in the hall," Gideon said. She had no idea when he'd gotten there. He had dust in his hair and blood on the side of his face, but he seemed to be okay.

Shay pushed past him. Taylor was standing in the hall, looking horrified and confused. She stared at Shay, who couldn't help but stare back.

"Taylor?" She asked, hesitantly.

"Who… you're Shay, right?" she asked. At least she knew her name, though Shay didn't know if it was because Gideon had told her or not. "Is it over?"

"I think so?" Shay said. "Yeah. I mean, the tear is closed and she's…gone, isn't she?"

"Good, we need to get out of here," Gideon said. "Now. We broke into a historic landmark and messed up the fence real good. I know it was the ghost, but I don't think the cops are going to see it that way."

"We broke into here?" Taylor's voice cracked. She reached into her pocket and pulled out a set of keys. "Are you sure?"

"Oh, well, we didn't break in here, then," Gideon said. "But we're going to want to leave anyway."

"Back to Jo's?" Max suggested.

"Probably the safest place," Jo agreed. "Come on, Taylor, we'll get you home."

"Wait." Taylor grabbed Shay's hand. "She…she told me something. Before she left. A message for you."

"What?" Shay asked.

"She said when you're ready, you'll need to find her," Taylor said. "I don't…I don't know what that means…I…"

She burst into tears.

"C'mon, Tay, it's okay." Gideon wrapped an arm around her and she sobbed into his shoulder. "Let's get going. It's going to be all right."

Shay wasn't sure exactly when she fell asleep. Somewhere along the way back to Spellbound. She didn't even remember getting into the car.

When she woke up it felt like it had been too long and not long enough.

She was lying in the bed of the guest room. She recognized the furniture. Light spilled through the window, clean and warm. Everything smelled like lavender, and for the moment it was quiet. A breeze made the trees outside her window whisper conspiratorially to each other. Soon, the leaves would be gone.

She sat up and rubbed the side of her head. Someone had taken out her braid, probably Max. Someone else had gotten her into pajamas. Probably Jo.

She felt grimy and awful, with no idea how long she'd been asleep.

The door opened and Max stepped in. They stopped when they saw her. "Oh! You're awake!"

"I guess." Talking made her feel like she'd spent the entire time she was asleep gargling sand. She was so grateful to see them that if she'd had the energy for it, she would have cried.

"Let me get you some water. Don't move."

She wasn't sure how much moving she could do. Her right hand, the one she'd used to punch the ghost, was heavily bandaged and in a splint. Her ankle was wrapped. Her throat felt horribly constricted and her ribs all hated her.

Max was back a moment later with a bottle of water. "Here. Drink this, slowly. We called a doctor and he looked you over, so uh, sorry about that, but it had been a few hours and you weren't waking up so…"

"It's okay, Max, thanks." She took a sip of the water. It hurt to swallow, but it felt like heaven.

"Yeah. He said you're really lucky. Just bruises mostly, though you did sprain your wrist pretty badly." Max smiled a bit. "I um. I'm sorry, Shay. I was…well, okay, we can talk about that later."

"No, we're talking about it," Shay said. She was so grateful to see them, very obviously them with no weird accent that didn't belong in their mouth. "It's not your fault you were possessed or… or drained by a ghost, or…you are okay, right?"

"Seriously? You're asking me?" Max's eyes looked a little bright and their voice was a little shaky. "You gave me the scare of a lifetime, like I seriously probably have gray hairs from that, and you're asking if I'm okay? I'm fine. Totally fine. I don't remember being possessed so…I'm good. I'm just…I'm really glad you're okay."

"Yeah." She started. "Wait. What about Finnias? And Arlo? Did we figure that out?"

"Um, maybe I should wait…"

"Max."

"Shay." They sighed. "I should probably let Duncan-"

"She's awake!" As if he was summoned, Duncan barged into the room. He practically ran to the bed and hugged her, thankfully gently. "Oh man, ShayShay, I thought that our parents were going to kill me. I thought you were dead. I am so glad you're alive."

"Glad you're alive too, Donuts," Shay said. "You seem fine."

Duncan sat on her other side. "I seem awesome, because I am. So. You look like crap."

"I feel like crap," she said. "What happened?"

"Okay, so, Finnias left me, and then the tear closed," Duncan said. "You were awake for a bit, but I don't know if you remember it, you were out pretty fast after that. Finn's been MIA ever since, which is, well, I dunno how I feel about that. Prob cause he helped you close the tear. So. That's a thing I'm gonna deal with later. Haven't found Arlo, so that's also a thing that we're working on now. Obviously Not Taylor is still at large, wherever she is. Actual Taylor says the last few months are pretty fuzzy, so that's fun. Uhhhh it really hasn't been that long, so that's about all the updates I have. Oh! But our apartment mostly didn't burn down so I was able to salvage a bunch of our crap. We're staying here until things calm down. Jo insisted."

"Shouldn't things be calmed down?" Shay asked.

"Ah, okay, that's the other update," Duncan said. "So I'm sure you remember blowing up the big ghost thing."

"I remember," she said.

"Yeah. Displaced a whole bunch of ghosts. They're still around, milling about in places they aren't supposed to be. And they're not very happy about it. The phone has been ringing off the hook with people needing ghost removal."

Max sighed. "We agreed to wait to tell her that."

"Yeah, but, it's part of the whole update package and I waited at least two minutes." Duncan shrugged. "Anyway, Jo needs all the help she can get and I guess that's us, now. Well, mostly you. Gotta pay rent somehow, am I right? Plus she's pretty sure you're the key to finding Arlo."

"Someone named Archibald has him," Shay said. "…A ghost. A ghost named Archibald has him. I don't know how, or where. But…"

Max put an arm around her and she leaned against them. They were warm and solid. Things felt normal, just for a moment.

"Well, that's news, at least." Duncan sighed. "But yeah, we kind of owe her, so I guess helping her out however we can is the least we can do."

"We kinda hecked it up, yeah," Shay agreed.

"I mean, we saved Taylor," Max said. "And you closed the tear. That's probably good for humanity as a whole. And especially Teton Falls."

"Yay." Shay didn't feel very accomplished.

Max patted her shoulder, gently. "I'm serious. I'm super proud of you."

She was having a hard time being proud of herself. "Thanks. Oh, your necklace-"

She put a hand to her throat, but it was gone.

"I put it in your jewelry holder," Max said. "You should keep it."

"Are you sure?" Shay asked. "But you…"

She couldn't say it.

"I can get another one," Max said. "If it helped, even a little bit, then you should keep it."

She didn't know what to say. Even if she could have found the words, she doubted she could have forced them out.

"Shay, I-"

They were going to apologize, she knew they were. She shook her head, a little too hard. It made her feel dizzy. "I'm gonna go shower."

"Okay. I put your clothes away, in the dresser. So um. Plenty of clothes." Max stood up and helped her to her feet. "Do you need any help?"

"No, I've got this," she said. She hurt all over, but her ankle didn't hurt nearly as bad as it had. "Thanks, Max."

She barely glanced in the mirror before her shower. She knew exactly what she looked like – a half dead raccoon that had been rolling around in some grease, probably. The hot water felt amazing, and she found she didn't mind the lavender as much now. Maybe Jo was onto something, there was something soothing about it.

Once she was dressed she braced herself and wiped down the mirror.

She still looked bad. She had dark circles around her eyes and the bruises around her neck formed a macabre necklace. She brushed her fingers through her hair.

Her skin pulled back and disappeared.

"Well, okay, I don't look that bad," she said. "I guess I did make a promise, didn't I."

She waved and her reflection was a little slow to wave back.

"Hey mirror ghost," she said. "What's shaking?"

The skeleton in the mirror used a bony finger to write on the inside of the glass, the letters appearing like the surface fogged over again. The message was backwards, but easy enough to read.

I know where Arlo is.

Before she could react, the ghost kept writing.

Finnias needs you.

"Oh," she said. "That's what's shaking."

Acknowledgements

Writing a book always feels like a solitary endeavor, but looking back there are so many people who helped me along the way that I have to thank them.

First of all, a huge shout out to my beta readers and hype girls Brooklyn and Jennifer. You two are the best, and definitely keep me motivated!

To my writer's group, Gene, Sarah, and Mikaela for always listening to me ramble on about ghosts and the characters, and always being willing to read an excerpt.

Katie, Yoko, and Anne for always being excited to hear more.

My fabulous roommate, Colleen, for her continued support.

Everyone at Cloaked Press for making this possible. Thank you so much for all of your work!

To Carmilla for the amazing cover and yelling about cryptids with me.

A huge and special thank you to my dear friend, Cindy, who heard the concept and told me to write it, and for still getting excited every time I talk about it.

To everyone who encouraged me to keep the title Ghost Punch.

And last, but certainly not least, thank you for reading! I hope to see you all for the sequel, That's the Spirit!

A. Lawrence

www.ingramcontent.com/pod-product-compliance
Lightning Source LLC
Chambersburg PA
CBHW061548210726
48287CB00006B/2113